"You know, when I was young, my mother used to kiss my cuts and bruises to make me feel better," Chase said playfully.

"Really," Nikita replied.

He nodded. "Yes, really," he said softly.

"Did it work? Did you feel better?"

His smile was pure seduction. "Immeasurably."

Nikita leaned in close. He lowered his head. She could see the anticipation in his eyes. "Then perhaps you should call your mother," she whispered.

He laughed out loud, then stepped back and continued chuckling. When he finally stopped, he looked at her and smiled. "You're different than I expected."

"What exactly did you expect?"

"I'm not really sure…just different."

The rain began to let up, which meant she was leaving. His eyes focused on her. The seriousness of his expression unnerved her. She took a step back. He smiled, knowing he was affecting her.

"Good night. Take care of that cut," she said, then turned to leave. But she didn't get far. Chase grabbed and held her hand. She turned as he pulled her into his arms. Her body slammed against his. A tiny gasp escaped. An instant later, his mouth came down on hers, taking her breath away. With her lips already parted, he slipped his tongue between them. He tasted like pure heaven.

Books by Celeste Norfleet

Kimani Romance

Sultry Storm
When It Feels So Right
Cross My Heart
Flirting with Destiny
Come Away with Me
Just One Touch
Just One Taste

CELESTE O. NORFLEET

is a native Philadelphian who has always been artistic, but now her artistic imagination flows through the computer keys instead of a paintbrush. She is a prolific writer for the Kimani Arabesque and Kimani Romance lines. Her romance novels, realistic with a touch of humor, depict strong sexy characters with unpredictable plots and exciting story lines. With an impressive backlist, she continues to win rave reviews and critical praise for her spicy sexy romances that scintillate, as well as entertain. Celeste also lends her talent to the Kimani TRU young adult line. Her young adult novels are dramatic fiction, reflecting current issues facing all teens. Celeste has been nominated and is the winner of numerous awards. Celeste lives in Virginia with family. You can visit her website, www.celesteonorfleet.wordpress.com, or contact her at conorfleet@aol.com or P.O. Box 7346, Woodbridge, VA 22195-7346.

Just One Taste

CELESTE O. NORFLEET

KIMANI™
ROMANCE

To Fate & Fortune

Recycling programs
for this product may
not exist in your area.

ISBN-13: 978-0-373-86266-5

JUST ONE TASTE

Printed in U.S.A.

Dear Reader,

Thank you so much for your continued support. It's a true pleasure to bring you the fourth book in the Coles family series. In *Just One Taste,* I reintroduce you to Nikita Coles of Key West. But this story comes with a twist. Nikita's love interest is Chase Buchanan, a member of the Buchanan family of Alaska.

Nikita sees trouble as soon as Chase comes to town, but their attraction is too tempting to resist. From the very first chapter, the characters burn right through the pages. Their first kiss sets the stage to a heated romance, and the hot and sexy love scenes keep the passion going to the end.

I hope you enjoy reading the love story of Nikita and Chase as they come together to find lasting love in *Just One Taste*.

Watch for more Coles family and Buchanan family series novels, coming soon.

Enjoy!

Celeste O. Norfleet

www.celesteonorfleet.wordpress.com

Chapter 1

"Chef."

Nikita Coles looked up as Russ, the waiter, paused briefly before he exited the kitchen. She spared a quick glance at his tray of delectable delights. Her dark brown eyes sparkled with pride as she examined the succulent bite-size morsels. *Perfect.* She nodded her approval and he hurried out the kitchen door to the dining room and waiting guests. She spared a moment to look around. Today had been crazy, but she'd actually done it. Two events in one evening and to her credit both had been perfectly planned and executed.

Because of her early hours at the café, she didn't usually take weekday catering jobs, let alone two in one evening. But this last one was special. It was at her older brother Mikhail's home and he had asked her to do this as a favor. While he was overseas, he'd rented his home out to a business associate and asked her to cater this event in his absence. She agreed. So after setting up, cooking and supervising the first event, she hurried here to the second job of the evening.

The kitchen hummed with the harmony of a well-orchestrated symphony. Every instrument fit perfectly and everyone knew their job and performed it expertly. Leroy, the sous chef, prepped and readied the food, she cooked and prepared the plates and Russ served the guests. What probably looked like disheveled confusion was actually perfectly planned and controlled chaos, which would result in two successful events. She had pulled together an exceptional team and knew that when she left the first job, everything would continue exactly the same in her absence.

But the long hours were starting to take their toll on her. It was getting late and she was exhausted and wanted to go home. She looked at her watch, then went back to wrapping dessert packages. All she needed now was for this job to be done.

"I'm here."

Nikita glanced up a brief second upon hearing her friend and business manager, Darcy Richardson's, voice as she hurried into the kitchen. "Hey, what are you doing here?" she tossed over her shoulder without turning around completely.

"I stopped by to see if you needed any last-minute help."

"The only thing I need is for them to leave," Nikita said, nodding toward the dining-room door. "They've been huddled talking all night."

"Well, they'd better hurry up. It's starting to rain and it looks like it's gonna get really bad out there. The wind's picking up and you know what that means— we're in for a crazy, stormy night. I know they say it's just the tail end of a tropical storm, but it sure feels like a whole lot more to me."

"I just have to finish wrapping these take-home desserts. We'll be out of here long before it starts getting really bad," Nikita assured her as she continued wrapping desserts and placing them on the tray.

"Good," Darcy said, walking to the counter to see what Nikita was doing. "You know how the roads around here flood in just an inch of rain. And don't even get me started on the falling trees."

"Yeah, I know," Nikita said, then finally glanced up again. "Whoa, check you out. You look great. I know you didn't have that on earlier at the Bentleys'. Where are you going tonight?"

"I had to change into something more appropriate. I have a date later this evening. You like?" She struck a classic fashion pose. Leroy, the sous chef, whistled and in pure vanity mode, Darcy smiled from ear to ear. "Thank you, darling," she said with her throaty Southern drawl that would've put Scarlett O'Hara to shame. She turned to a large shiny pan sitting on the counter, looked at her reflection and checked her makeup.

Nikita just shook her head and chuckled. Darcy was incorrigible at times—apparently this was going to be one of them.

A retired model, Darcy was tall and thin with bleached-blond hair styled in a perfectly coiffed French braid. She was dressed in a white single-button pantsuit cut low in front, minus anything underneath, and five-inch stiletto sandals. Her makeup was flawless and of course her smile sparkled. Compared to Nikita, dressed in her white cook's jacket, jeans and comfortable flats, Darcy looked like a shimmering gemstone.

She had her Prada evening clutch and bedazzled cell phone in one hand and a check and a bottle of champagne in the other. "This is for you, darling—compliments of Mr. and Mrs. Woodrow Bentley III. They loved the food, especially the desserts, and along with their guests, they came into the kitchen to meet you. I relayed your sincere apologies."

"Thank you," Nikita said, then looked at the bottle and the check. "I'll take the check."

Darcy smiled happily. "Good, I was hoping you'd say that. Oh, and here," she began as she dug into her clutch, "you left this at the Bentleys'." She pulled out a cell phone. "I swear you must be exhausted. I've never known you to leave your phone behind at a job before. And seriously, I don't know how you did it today— up and at the café by four in the morning, working all morning and afternoon and then acing two catering jobs this evening."

"It's all for the greater goal," Nikita said proudly.

"Still, I will never set up another double booking in one night again. I can't believe it's only just Tuesday." She inhaled deeply. "Mmm, it smells like heaven in here. What was for dinner? I'm starved," she said, looking around.

"I thought you said you have a date tonight."

"I do, but you know I can't eat when I'm on a date. I just order a salad and water with lemon. Guys like that."

Nikita chuckled, shaking her head again. "We served grilled salmon with a light lemon and caper sauce, smashed potatoes and sautéed asparagus and shallots in white wine."

Darcy took the offered plate of food from the sous chef and began securing an equal amount of everything onto her fork. Then slipping it into her mouth, she closed her eyes and moaned lovingly. "I swear I have no idea how you do it every time. This food is smack-your-mama delicious. I can't wait until you expand the café into the space next door. With your cooking skills and my connections, it's gonna be fabulous."

"I certainly hope so," Nikita said optimistically. "With all the catering referrals from my two sisters' weddings and the lucrative personal chef jobs you've booked for me recently, I just about have enough money to pay off my mortgage outright, make a serious down payment on the building next door, then connect the two together. The designs are already drawn up, and I have an appointment with Wendy at the real-estate office next week."

"You know you could have secured the building years ago. I have some money from my trust fund and I know your family would have helped out."

Nikita shook her head. "No, I couldn't do that. Suppose it didn't work and went belly-up? I would have lost everybody's money and I couldn't do that to you or my family, no matter how much you all insisted. No," she said definitively, "I needed to do this on my own and

I did. So, now that I almost have enough, I can focus solely on expanding the café."

"Okay, I'll make a note. No more private chef jobs."

"Actually, maybe one or two more jobs. Remodeling never goes like it's supposed to, so a little extra cash won't hurt."

Darcy shook her head. "Girl, you and I both know you're sitting on a gold mine with your cottage and land out on Stock Island. How many offers have you had recently—a dozen? That place is worth a fortune. All you have to do is sell it and cash in. You know you didn't even want it before."

Nikita smiled. Darcy was right. When her ex-fiancé, Reed Blackwell, presented her with the cottage instead of an engagement ring, she was thrilled. Then when she saw it she was stunned. The place was a run-down shack that had been abandoned and neglected for years. She didn't really want it before but she also knew that she'd never sell it.

The cottage was her badge of endurance. She had loved Reed and he had betrayed her. A part of her still wanted to get back at him, and keeping the cottage was doing just that. She had intended to sign it over to Reed years ago, but his family's threats and demands had soon ended that notion. Now she was going to keep it until she wanted to let it go. "You're right. I didn't want it at first, but now I do want it. There's no way I'm gonna sell it."

"And when they double the real-estate taxes?" Darcy asked.

"Then I'll just figure something else out."

Darcy nodded. "Okay, I'll see what private chef jobs I can come up with."

"So how did the Bentley party finish out?"

"Flawless, as usual," Darcy said. "I was the last one out, and the place was spotless."

Nikita knew it would be, particularly with Darcy's slight touch of obsessive-compulsive disorder when it came to cleanliness and organization. "Good, thanks."

Russ hurried in and looked around. "Are they almost done in there?" Darcy asked him.

He nodded. "Yep, in a few minutes. They're ready for the—"

Nikita instantly handed him a tray of wrapped desserts. He grabbed it, then hurried out again. Nikita went to the sink, washed her hands and turned back to Darcy. "Leroy's almost finished with the pots and pans and I just have to load the dishwasher when the rest of the dessert dishes come back." She looked around. "This is my brother's home, so I really need to make sure everything's perfect when I leave."

"The kitchen will be immaculate as usual. And I gotta tell you, girl, if the rest of the house is anything like this kitchen, this house needs to be photographed for *Architectural Digest*. It's breathtaking."

"Actually it has been in a couple of magazines, including *Architectural Digest*. But you know I still can't believe Mikhail rented it out like this. He's never done that before. I asked my sisters and no one's even heard Mikhail mention Chase Buchanan before."

"Hmm, now talk about mouthwatering. Chase Buchanan is tall, gorgeous and built like a warrior. You

know who he is, right? His family owns Titan Energy
Corporation—the largest African American–owned
energy company in the United States. They're the ones
who bought the huge Blackwell property on Stock Island
a few months ago."

Nikita nodded her head. "Yeah, I heard. To tell you
the truth, I'm surprised the Blackwells sold it. They always said it was their family legacy."

"Well, not anymore. Money talks and I hear everyone and everything has a price tag. Rumor has it they're
going to build some kind of research facility out there."

"Nah, they're probably gonna build an oil refinery
and pollute the air, and then destroy the entire ecosys-
tem in the process. My cottage and the land will be
worthless."

Darcy chuckled at Nikita's extreme assessment.
"Come on, I don't think it's gonna be that bad. But you
know you could always just sell it to Titan. The cottage
is right beside their property, isn't it?"

"Yeah, but the cottage sits on less than two acres of
land. That's nothing compared to the Blackwell property. What's two acres compared to over fifty?"

"Still, I'm surprised Titan hasn't tried to buy it from
you."

"They have. I keep turning them down. They have
what they want. I'm sure they don't need my little two-
acre cottage. It's totally insignificant. Besides, I'd never
sell to an oil company."

"Did you meet him yet?" Darcy asked.

"Buchanan?" Nikita asked. Darcy nodded. "No, I
spoke with his assistant when I arrived, and after that

I was too busy." Nikita grabbed her backpack. She dug out her small leather-bound journal and began writing. She'd altered the sauce of the salmon and wanted to make a notation in her recipe book. This was where she kept all of her work-in-progress recipes.

Darcy quickly finished her food then took one of the extra chocolate desserts on the counter and popped it into her mouth. She closed her eyes and allowed the sinful sensation to slowly melt down her throat. "Oh, my God, this is insanely delicious," she moaned. "What is it?"

"Something I've been playing around with. It's a bite-size chocolate parfait cup filled with spiced dark chocolate ganache layered atop chocolate mousse and topped with crumbled chocolate-covered cocoa beans. What do you think? You like?"

"Are you kidding? It's so good I swear it's damn near orgasmic."

Nikita chuckled and shook her head. Darcy was a bona fide chocoholic with a supersonic metabolism. She could eat anything and never gain an ounce. "*Orgasmic* is an interesting description. I like it. Maybe that's what I'll call them—mini orgasms."

Darcy laughed. "So how'd it go out there earlier?" Darcy asked.

"Like piranhas on a feeding frenzy," Nikita joked. "The food was disappearing as fast as we were getting it out there. I've never seen people eat so fast. Four of the guests even asked for seconds. Thankfully we came prepared."

"You're a hit, darling."

"Or maybe they were just hungry."

"I don't think so. It's the food. They love it. They love you and you know they're gonna want to meet you. They always do at these private dinner parties," Darcy said as she walked over to the kitchen door to peek out into the dining room.

"No thanks. I need to get this place cleaned up then get out of here. My alarm clock goes off in—" she paused to glance at her watch "—seven hours, and I need to be in bed for at least five of them. Besides, schmoozing with our clientele is your job, not mine." Along with her other responsibilities, as business manager for her café, Darcy ran interference when it came to situations like this. She was responsible for dealing with café customers and catering clients. She had the personality for it and thankfully enjoyed doing it. "I just cook the food, remember?"

"You do a hell of a lot more than that," Darcy said, returning to the island across from Nikita who was drying and putting the pots and pans away. Since it was her brother's home she knew where everything went. "See, case in point—look at these dinner plates. Rich people don't eat everything on their plates. It's some kind of rich rule. But look at this plate. I swear it looks like it's been licked clean. See, even the design is eaten off."

Nikita laughed. Darcy was a character and she could always depend on her to lighten her mood.

"Actually, Nikita, it might be a good idea to concede this one time and step out to get your accolades. I just peeked out in the dining room and the guest list is a who's who in local and state politics. The mayor, a couple of city commissioners, a state congressman and two prominent attorneys are all out there, enjoying your food. Think of the future catering connections."

Nikita stopped what she was doing and looked at Darcy curiously. Darcy knew powerful people, so when she said major political players were in the dining room, you could bet she wasn't mistaken.

Chase Buchanan smiled dutifully as those around him talked nonstop. The conversations centered mainly on Titan, the business, the product and its future endeavors in the south Florida area. In his presence, few spoke about anything else. Money and power had a way of doing that. And Titan Energy Corporation had money and power in abundance. Everybody wanted inside information like what was next for the multibillion-dollar corporation. Of course, he never disclosed anything. Still, catering to him was a necessity. Now he just expected it. When he called, they came, when he spoke they listened and when he said jump, they did.

"They" being the wannabe rich and powerful who felt being in his presence gave them meager entrance to the club to which they so fervently wanted to belong. They were wrong, of course. Titan's inner circle and the Buchanan family were close-knit and impossible to penetrate. The only way into the Titan family was through the Buchanan name.

It wasn't exactly arrogance that assured him of this. It was years of experience. He'd seen them come and go. Businessmen, politicians, women, all wanted to get close to him and gain entrance into the inner sanctum of

Titan. The sad truth was they never had a chance. Birth or marriage was the only way in and the Buchanan men were known to be extremely selective.

He looked around, taking in the faces smiling for his benefit. He'd been at this job long enough to know human nature and what made people tick. Sitting here now gave him the perfect opportunity to affirm the obvious. Politicians and businessmen were a staple in his life. Right now he was only half paying attention as they exalted Titan's business and marketing proficiency. Since his arrival here this morning that was all he'd heard. After a while he'd stopped listening.

He had every intention of ending this monotonous evening early, but as usual, politicians needing money wanted as much face time as possible. They talked and touted their egos and abilities like prized pigs at a country fair, each with one desperate goal—to please him and dig down as far into his deep pockets as they could. It was a pathetic show of grandeur, which usually bored him. As always, tonight he dealt with it with his usual placid expression.

After all, he was a Buchanan. That meant being tolerant, composed and in control at all times. These ideologies were indoctrinated into him as far back as he could remember. He had taken that creed to the extreme.

Thus, the interminable evening droned on well past eight and seemed to threaten to go even later. He played his part as always, nodding when appropriate, smiling when called for and even giving a knowledgeable sound bite when absolutely necessary. But tonight wasn't about this meeting or these men sitting around the dining-room table ego-blasting themselves. It was ultimately about a woman in the kitchen who had something he wanted.

The Titan Research and Development advance team had been here for the past seven months. They'd acquired the property on which to build the Titan research facility, but had unfortunately run into an eleventh-hour problem. He'd been called in to finish the job. This was what he did, his specialty. He smoothed rough edges and got projects completed, and then he moved on to the next job.

"So, Chase," Oren Davis, Key West's top-rated Realtor and city appropriations commissioner, said with more zest then necessary, "is this really your first trip to Key West?"

"Yes, it is," Chase said.

"What are your plans while you're here in our fair city?"

Chase smiled. Here we go—the inevitable money pitch. "I'm just passing through. I don't intend to be here that long—just a few weeks. I'll finish the job and move on."

"Yes, but you must have some downtime planned. The evenings and weekends, perhaps?" Oren queried.

"I intend to be too busy working."

"Too busy working? Nonsense! No, no, we can't have that, can we, boys?" he stated while looking around at the other men seated at the table now more interested in the dessert than the conversation. "While you're here you should be entertained, perhaps see some of the delights of our beautiful city. I have the perfect companion for you."

Chase chuckled inside. He was wrong. This wasn't a money pitch—it was a matrimony pitch. Neither of which he was interested in. "I'm sure I'll be too busy, Mr. Davis," he said, glancing over to the waiter who immediately disappeared into the kitchen area.

"Well, we can't have you here in the city all alone. Now, my daughter is available to take you around and of course she'll take good care of you."

"Thank you, Mr. Davis, I'm sure I'll get around just fine."

"No trouble at all. I'll have my daughter stop by."

Chase's associate, Kelvin Simmons, cleared his throat and pushed his chair back. "Chase, thank you. This was a delightful evening. I hadn't realized how late it was getting. I'm afraid I'm going to have to push on."

Several of the other men at the table immediately followed suit. Moments later everyone was standing and extolling their gratitude to their host. The waiter came back in with a tray of wrapped desserts.

Chase smiled as each man shook his hand while repeating their willingness to offer their services and giving him yet another business card for his growing pile. He played his part and smiled graciously. He was impatient by nature, but he'd long since learned to appear calm and interested. His mother referred to it as his aggressive Buchanan genes overruling her calmer recessive genes. So he learned to take his time in most things.

Several of the men still mingled around, talking. Oren Davis made a point of standing by his side as each man passed, then he stepped up quickly. "Chase, perhaps you and I could speak privately."

"Regarding?"

"I understand you're having trouble acquiring the last Blackwell property. As the top Realtor in this area, I'd be happy to lend my assistance and expertise."

"Titan has people who handle that."

"Yes, of course, but I'd be happy to expedite any problems. Perhaps we can discuss this in greater detail when the others depart."

"Actually, I'm expecting a few phone calls later this evening."

"Of course, of course. Perhaps we can get together another time. I'll have my office contact your associate and we'll set up a time."

Chase nodded without being totally committed. His calm, unhurried facade was about to crack. He might appear relaxed but inside he was anxious to get this job done and get out of here. The tediousness of this production, although necessary, was frustrating. But now it was time to attend to the business he came here to do.

From the corner of his eye he saw the waiter looking toward the kitchen. He turned, following the man's line of vision, and saw her, Nikita Coles, peeking out the kitchen door. He knew his effect on women. They adored him instantly. But it appeared she didn't smile as most women did upon seeing him. She just stared. Apparently, she wasn't going to be like most women. A part of him liked that idea. Most times it was too easy. Everything he read about her showed that she was a strong woman with intense beliefs and a stubborn nature for a just cause. It had been a long time since he ran into any type of business opposition.

He hoped she would be more of a challenge. He smiled. She didn't.

He nodded. She nodded. Perhaps she would be.

Chapter 2

Chase Buchanan. Of course his reputation preceded him. With men like Chase it usually did. Nikita had looked him up online before she got to her brother's house—something she did all the time with a new client. She never went into a situation without knowing as much about as many of the major players as she could. And this was one of those times. It helped that he was recently in the local newspaper, so she didn't have to look far.

She found out that Chase was a powerhouse player in the oil business. He worked overseas mainly, which made her curious as to why he was here in Key West. Still nothing she could find specified exactly what kind of work he did.

"Check it out," Darcy told her. "He's even got Oren Davis, the king of Key West real estate, out there. I bet he's on the hunt for a husband for another one of his daughters."

"Yeah, maybe, but he's also a city commissioner. That's a lot of high-powered political backing out there," Nikita said.

Darcy ate another dessert. "You know that's how things get done. It used to be the golf courses, but now it's over dinner and drinks. Hey, maybe Buchanan's going to run for local office."

Nikita shook her head. "Not likely. He's a Buchanan and that means oil and money run through his body instead of blood. And that also means that whatever brings him here has everything to do with making more money."

"You know they're buying up more land all over the city, too."

"Yeah, I know. I heard. Titan is going to take over the city pretty soon."

"Buchanans everywhere. Now wouldn't that be nice."

Nikita shook her head. "You have a one-track mind."

Darcy nodded. "Well at least they'll bring jobs to the area."

"Yeah, that's true, but still. I can just imagine a huge oil refinery right in my backyard. Every time I go to the cottage I'm gonna see a big ugly monstrosity looming behind my garden."

"Maybe it's not gonna be that bad," Darcy said.

"Doesn't matter."

"You can always sell it to them."

"I'm not that nice."

"Nikita, maybe you should. You can use that money to expand the café and make it exactly like you want it."

Nikita shook her head. "I'm not selling out to an oil company."

"Still, you don't know what they're gonna build."

"I guess I can always find out."

"How?" Darcy asked.

"Simple. I'll ask."

Darcy laughed. "Somehow I don't think that's gonna work. I can't see Titan or the Buchanans opening up and telling you what their plans are. Maybe if you ask nicely," Darcy said.

"Hmm, maybe I will."

"I was joking, Nikita. We're just going to have to wait and find out like everyone else." She popped another dessert into her mouth. "Oh, man, these are so good," she said, completely changing the subject. "You know I'd ask you for the recipe for these, but I know you won't give it to me. So have you thought about putting together another cookbook like I suggested last week? It would be fantastic. I'll even volunteer to be your taste tester. Hey, are you listening to me?"

Nikita had stopped paying attention. She knew about Titan buying the Blackwell property near her cottage. But what Reed and his family did had nothing to do with her. She was still thinking about the impressive guest list and why they were all here in her brother's home. "Yeah, I heard you, you want to taste test and I need to write another cookbook. I'll think about it. In the meantime…" She walked over to the kitchen door and curiously peeked out into the dining room again.

The guests were all standing around, talking and shaking hands. It looked as if the dinner party was indeed beginning to break up.

Nikita watched as each guest shook hands and spoke briefly with a man standing in the dining room archway. He smiled graciously and motioned toward Russ standing beside him with the tray of wrapped desserts. The guests each took one of the packages, and then headed to the foyer. So that was Chase Buchanan, she presumed.

Nikita could only see him in profile, but what she saw spiked her inner temperature. He was tall, easily over six feet, with a sleek, commanding build that made him stand out in a room. With firm, broad masculine shoulders, he seemed comfortably relaxed in the casual setting—commanding but not domineering. He had on a white shirt, a dark tie and a dark gray suit that was obviously tailored to fit him perfectly.

His jaw was chiseled firm and the upward curve of his full lips was seductively sensual. He was clean-shaven with a creamy caramel complexion that looked smooth and touchable. He turned and smiled, speaking to a guest. His eyes were green and seemed to shine in guarded awareness. Nikita licked her lips as her thoughts wandered in another direction. It had been too long and the man had *sexy* written all over him. A warm sensation eased through her body. A man like that would know exactly how to please a woman. She smiled again.

"That's him, Chase Buchanan. Look at his eyes, they're heavenly—green with golden specks," Darcy whispered into her ear. "He's got money, brains and he is gorgeous. Talk about a triple threat."

Nikita shrugged. "He's okay, if you want that type. Bottom line, he's just a man."

"Oh, please, darling. That's not just a man standing out there. That's *the* man. When's the last time you saw a man that looked like that? He's got it all. He's sexy, handsome, rich—and intelligent. Everybody wants that type. Remember, it's always about the sex."

Russ glanced in Nikita's direction. Chase turned around, following his line of vision. Their eyes locked for a brief moment. Nikita's stomach flinched and her heart jumped. His penetrating gaze held hers, then a slow easy smile curved his sexy full lips. It was as if he knew exactly what she'd been thinking. He nodded and she returned his gesture, then stepped back, closed the door and went back to the dishwasher.

"That's it? A nod? Nikita, the man is single as far as I know, gorgeous and rich," Darcy said following close behind.

"I don't have time for drama," Nikita said.

"Darling, you need your engines revved up and he looks like just the man to do it repeatedly." Darcy laughed at her own joke. "And who says he's gonna be drama?"

"Men like him are always drama."

"Well, if he's drama, you need a nice big slice of it."

"No thanks."

"Darling, you need this. Trust me."

"What I need is to get out of here."

"Chef."

Nikita turned, seeing Russ come into the kitchen with the last of the coffee and dessert dishes. He set the tray on the counter. "Umm, Mr. Buchanan would like to make a suggestion."

"A suggestion? What kind of suggestion?" she asked, beginning to stack the dishwasher again.

Russ, a college freshman working his way through school, looked around the kitchen, nervously stepping from foot to foot. "He thinks maybe if you'd add a bit more espresso to the ganache and some almond extract to the mousse, and then top the dessert with toasted almonds you'll have an added texture and a richer layer of flavoring."

"He suggested *what?*" Nikita stopped, totally stunned.

"Oh, crap," Darcy muttered, then glanced over to Leroy, who was leaning against the sink chuckling and shaking his head. "Okay, Russ, thanks for relaying the message," Darcy said quickly. "I'll make sure to tell Mr. Buchanan that we'll certainly consider his suggestion. In the meantime…"

Russ nodded with relief as he loosened his tie, knowing his shift was over. "Actually, no," Nikita said slowly, tensing with each word. Russ stopped. "Please go back out there and inform Mr. Buchanan that my desserts are perfect exactly as they are," she said firmly. "I do not need, nor do I want, his input on my cooking."

Russ looked around again.

"I have a better idea," Darcy interjected. "Russ, why don't you and Leroy just head on home. Nikita and I will finish up here."

Nikita looked at Darcy and immediately understood.

She nodded at Leroy and Russ. "Good idea. Good night, guys. Drive safely. I'll see you tomorrow."

They nodded and quickly grabbed their things and left.

Darcy turned to Nikita. "Are you okay?"

"Yeah, I'm fine. It's just been a long day and I'm tired and ready to go home."

"Why don't you go? I'll finish up here," Darcy said.

"No, you have a date, so you go ahead. I'll finish up here. I just have to fill the dishwasher and put the leftovers in the refrigerator. It won't take long."

"Are you sure?" Darcy asked.

"Yes, positive. Go, I'll see you tomorrow. Thanks for finishing up the Bentley job."

"No problem. I'll see you tomorrow. Behave yourself," Darcy warned sternly, then smiled and waved as she followed Russ and Leroy out the back door into the pouring rain.

Nikita stood there a moment shaking her head. Her temper and touchiness about her cooking would get the best of her one day. Thankfully, she had Darcy to keep her tempered. She looked around the empty kitchen. Large and extravagant, this was exactly as she'd planned when her brother had asked her to design it for him. Her thoughts quickly focused on the ideas she had for her new café kitchen. It would be perfect, if everything worked out like she planned. "Soon," she muttered, "but right now…" She turned quickly and her arm hit a dessert plate and brandy snifter, knocking them off the counter. They fell to the floor and shattered.

Chapter 3

Chase and Kelvin stood in the foyer just inside the doorway as torrential rain poured down in front of them. They discussed the evening's events as he watched the guests drive away. They came to the same conclusion, that it was a successful beginning. But Chase knew he had a long way to go to get his plans solidified. He made arrangements to follow up the next few days with a series of one-on-one meetings.

"How soon can we get the governor's team involved?" he asked as his cell phone rang. He pulled it out of his pocket and looked at the caller ID. It was Daniel Buchanan. He let it go to voice mail.

"The governor's tied down in legislation right now and has a governors' meeting in New York next week."

"Okay, set up an appointment for the week after. I want to meet with him as soon as possible."

"Before you head back to Alaska?" Kelvin asked.

"Yes," Chase said, checking his cell phone messages. "All right, that's it." Kelvin nodded. "Oh, one more thing, good job on getting the caterer. I'll see you tomorrow."

Kelvin nodded, turned and hurried to his car. He drove away. Moments later three more cars left from the back of the house. Chase stepped back inside and paused in the foyer to look around. This really was a stunning home. Six bedrooms, six baths, living room, dining room, library, office, exercise room, a game room and a few others he hadn't even bothered to check out. It was perfect for his short stay in the states. It was also just by chance that his half brother, Andre, knew Mikhail Coles and was able to secure a short-term residence for him while he was in Key West. The cell phone rang again. He answered, knowing exactly who it was. "Yes."

"Chase, did you see the location yet?" Daniel Buchanan asked abruptly, obviously not in the mood for basic phone pleasantries.

"Hello, Daniel. No, I haven't seen it yet."

"Why not?" he said heatedly. "What are you waiting for?"

"It's private property."

"It's on an island, not in the middle of Fort Knox. It's not like there's security. It's a shack in the middle of nowhere. You need to get out there and see it now," he ordered.

"Daniel, it's against the law," Chase said pointedly.

"Damn the law. Tell them you're a Buchanan."

Chase nearly laughed out loud. Daniel was a throwback relic from the arm-twisting days of the twenties when lawless racketeering, official bribing and blatant aggression ruled the land. "That might work in Alaska, but not in the real world with the rest of us. I follow the rules."

He huffed. "Fine, so what exactly are you doing?"

"I just purchased two buildings in town."

"Chase, we're supposed to be making money on this venture, not giving it away."

"We need leverage. This is it."

Daniel exhaled loudly with a deep grumble of annoyance. "All right, did you at least meet with the officials yet?"

"Yes. I met with them this evening. They just left. It went well. I don't think we'll have a problem should it become necessary to go in another direction."

"What do you mean 'should it be necessary'? You suggested initiating the process of eminent domain, I approved. I want you to go in another direction right now. We're on a nonnegotiable timetable here."

"I know our timetable, Daniel, and upon further review of the situation I don't believe that's a necessary option at this point." Chase knew full well Daniel's impatience. Daniel Buchanan would certainly not be considered a charmer. His idea of swatting a mosquito was to detonate a nuclear device. He was brash and impetuous and when he wanted something, he ran roughshod over anyone and everyone to get it. Titan was his only concern. He lived and breathed for the company and God help anyone who got in his way.

"Make it an option. This was your idea and it will

give us exactly what we need," Daniel ordered. "I want this finished now."

"Daniel, we have to be patient. This is going to be tricky enough and we need to move cautiously. The last thing we need is a PR nightmare, and after the Gulf oil spill in 2010, that's exactly what we'll get. Your way, bulldozing into submission, will not work in this case. We need to use finesse. The locals are already—"

"I don't give a damn about the locals. We can't let this opportunity slip by. Do you have any idea how many companies would love to step in and take over this project? No, this is too important to Titan. Perhaps your being in Europe the last few months has softened your edge and clouded your outlook on our goal. Apparently, you're not the uncompromising businessman you once were."

Chase visibly bristled. His jaw tightened and he shifted the phone against his ear. "Respectfully, Daniel," Chase began patiently, "my outlook has neither changed nor varied. You need to step back and allow me to get the job done the way I see fit. You had a problem, remember? Your way didn't work, so you called me. Not the other way around. I resolve problems. That's what I do."

"Well, you don't seem to be doing it right now," Daniel said.

Chase's eyes narrowed. "Don't taunt me, Daniel, and don't threaten me." His voice was stern and uncompromising. "Remember, I'm the last person you want to push too far." His words of warning sliced deep.

Daniel immediately backed down. "I need this done,

Chase," he said calmly. "I sent you in for one reason and one reason only."

"Either I handle this my way or I get back on my plane. You choose, right now." There was a noise in the house. Chase grimaced and turned around. Something had broken in the kitchen. As far as he knew he was in the house alone.

"Okay. Your way, and that's exactly the determined fire I want to hear in your voice," Daniel said. "I needed to make sure that the Chase I know is still up on his game. You keep that fire burning, son. Just make sure it works in Titan's favor. Call me next week with good news."

Chase ended the call and turned toward the kitchen. He walked through the foyer and dining room down the short hall to the kitchen door. He heard water running, but the room was empty when he opened the door. He scanned the kitchen more closely, knowing someone was there. Seconds later, Nikita Coles stood up with a brush and dustpan in her hands. She walked to a closet in the mudroom, came out and went to the sink.

Chase stood there watching her. Seeing her earlier had made him curious. Seeing her now piqued his interest. He'd observed her in photos, both on the internet and in the dossier he had on her. But they were nothing compared to her being there in person. She was medium height and slim with cinnamon-toasted skin. Her features were soft and delicate, dark almond-shaped eyes, and high cheekbones and full softly tinted lips. She was known as a brilliant and temperamental chef and also an intelligent businesswoman with an eye for future developments. The latter was what brought him here.

A knowing smile tipped his lips. Knowing everything about a person can sometimes take the fun out of getting to know them naturally. But this wasn't a typical get-to-know-you situation. This was business. She had something he wanted and within the next few weeks he intended to get it. But right now he needed to find a way to get close to her.

"Good evening," he said in a mellow voice.

Nikita turned quickly, obviously unaware that he'd been standing there watching her. "Hi," she said breathlessly, turning the water off. He started walking around the counter toward her. "No, don't come any closer," she warned. "There might still be broken glass on the floor."

He looked down, scanning the perfectly clean marble floor. "It looks like you got it all," he said, seeing the broom and mop leaning against the counter.

"Just in case, you'd better stay back. I'll take care of this."

"Are you sure you don't need a hand?"

"No. Thank you."

He nodded, realizing she obviously wanted to keep distance between them. He smiled. She seemed nervous to be here with him. This was perfect. Apparently, what he'd recently learned about her wasn't quite complete. He looked down on the floor again seeing two small pieces of glass a good distance from the sink. He walked over and bent down to pick them up. "You missed a couple."

"No, I got it," she said quickly, but he was already there. "Here, let me take that from you."

He stood up with the cut glass already cradled in the palm of his hand. "I have it. Trash can?" he asked. She pointed. He walked over, opened the lid and dropped the broken glass inside.

"Thank you. Please, by all means get back to your guests. I'll be out of your way shortly." She grabbed a towel and wiped the already perfectly clean island counter.

"My guests have already gone," he said casually as he moved closer, then stopped and leaned back against the counter beside her.

"Did they enjoy the meal?" she asked, moving to the sink.

He chuckled. "You know they did."

"And you?"

"Yes, I enjoyed it, too. You're a very talented chef."

"Thank you," she said, turning the water on and rinsing her hands.

"I'm sorry, where are my manners? My name is Chase Buchanan." He extended his hand to shake.

"I know who you are, Mr. Buchanan. Key West is a lot smaller than some people think. When a Buchanan from Titan Energy Corporation comes to town, word gets around fast."

"Yes, I suppose it would, and I also suppose you pay attention."

She nodded. "I'm Nikita Coles. Sorry, my hands are wet."

"That's okay." He grabbed a couple of paper towels and handed them to her.

"Thanks."

He nodded. "Then you also know I'm new in town and I was wondering if you—" he began, then stopped. She smiled and seemed to half chuckle. He was immediately curious. "What?" he asked.

"That's a really lame pick-up line," she said, drying her hands.

He smiled. "Yes, I guess it is, but I assure you I hadn't intended it to be. I don't do pick-up lines."

"Of course not. Sorry, I just thought—" She cut off her words as her cheeks burned with embarrassment. "Never mind. It was presumptuous of me to imply otherwise."

"No need to apologize," he said. "I'm sure you hear lame pick-up lines all the time. And I would be more than happy to oblige, perhaps another time."

"No, not necessary. You were saying…"

"I was saying, I'm new in town and I was wondering if you'd be willing to—" He stopped again and walked over to her looking very serious. "Are you bleeding?" he asked.

"No."

"Are you sure?" he asked. She held her hands up to show him. There were no cuts and no blood. He slipped the paper towels he'd given her from her hands and held it up. There was a bloodstain on it. "Then where did this come from?"

"*You're* bleeding," Nikita said and quickly grabbed his arm and pulled him to the sink. She turned the water on and moved his hand under the cool stream, inspecting his hand for the wound. When she found a cut on his forefinger, she removed his hand from the water to examine the cut more closely. "Okay, it doesn't look too bad."

Chase watched as she carefully touched around the cut checking it closely. Her quick, immediate actions took him off guard at first, but now he was impressed and even liked it. "Are you sure?" he asked.

"Yes, believe me I've had my share of kitchen cuts, burns and bruises. This doesn't look too bad at all."

"So you think I'll survive? No stitches?" he joked again.

"No, I don't think you'll need stitches. But if you'd feel better, I'll drive you to the hospital. My brother Dominik is an E.R. surgeon at Key West Medical Center."

Of course he already knew that. "Actually, Ms. Coles, I was just joking with you." He smiled and watched as she turned and looked up into his eyes, lips slowly parting. His body tightened. A flood of burning desire cut through his center and pooled in his loins. She opened her mouth to say something but nothing came out. They just stared at each other a few seconds. Neither moved an inch. He began to think about all the things he could do right now. Kissing her topped the list. He didn't know about her, but it was getting hot and his body was about to combust.

Nikita swallowed hard. Suddenly, the simple act of cleaning a cut became an intimate interaction. She stood in front of the sink and he stood right behind her with his hand nearly around her waist. Her body was right there. They were almost connected.

Heavenly. Darcy was right. His eyes were heavenly. Green with specks of gold, they seemed to look right though her into her soul, touching her inner core of desires. She wasn't the kind of woman that waited patiently for things to happen. She made them happen. If she wanted something, she went out and got it. So for her to feel the least bit timid about wanting this man was out of character. But something inside of her warned her off. She heeded that.

She took a deep breath and looked away. "I need to… There's a…" she began, and then paused. "There's a first-aid kit under the sink. I'll get something for this." She knelt down in front of him and opened the cabinet door. In the guise of searching for the very obvious first-aid kit, she took a moment to calm her nerves, inhaling slowly and releasing a long, cleansing breath. She grabbed the plastic case. When she stood up she looked into his eyes again. Big mistake. She saw something she knew would take this in another direction. She quickly looked away and focused on his cut.

She washed and rinsed his cut again, then dried it. She squeezed antiseptic on his finger, then wrapped an appropriate-size Band-Aid snugly around his finger. "All right, I'm done."

"So, do you think I'll live?" he said.

"Yeah, you'll live," she said, knowing he was joking.

He looked at his finger. "It looks pretty good. Thanks."

"You're welcome."

"Umm, can I ask you a question?" she asked.

"Sure, you can ask."

"Why are you here?"

"Here, as in on planet Earth, or as in Key West?"

"In Key West," she specified.

He smiled. "I'm not in the habit of discussing Titan business with those other than the Buchanan family. Being a major energy company, any information can be construed and used for ill-gotten gains such as insider trading."

"Oh, of course, I understand. Company secrets. Okay, it's late and I've gotta get out of here."

"Are you sure? It's still raining pretty hard out there."

She nodded. "Yes, I'll be fine. I need to go," she said tightly. "I have a date with a—"

"A date?" he asked quickly, apparently taken off guard. "I didn't realize you were…"

She half smiled. "Yes, I have a date with my alarm clock. It goes off at three in the morning. I have pastries to make and a café to open by six o'clock."

"Ah, that's right, Nikita's Café."

"You should stop by sometime," she said, grabbing her jacket and backpack on her way to the back door.

"I will," he promised.

"It was interesting meeting you," she said.

"It was a pleasure meeting you."

Chase followed her to the mudroom and opened the back door for her. The rain poured down in steady sheets. Nikita stood beside him looking out. Even seeing across the driveway to the wooded area was nearly impossible. There was no way she could drive home safely in this.

As if he read her thoughts, he turned back to her. "There's no way I can let you leave here in this."

She nodded. "It'll pass in a few minutes," she said, hoping she was right. Being here with him, this close, was starting to test her resolve. Darcy was right. It was about the sex.

"So, Ms. Coles, what does one cook for a chef?"

She looked at him. "What?"

"For dinner, for breakfast, for lunch, what does someone cook for a chef?"

"Simple is always best."

"Cinnamon toast with bananas and chocolate," he suggested.

She looked at him questioningly. Few people outside of her family knew that she loved cinnamon toast with bananas and chocolate. "I think you know a lot more about me than you let on," she said suspiciously.

"I confess," he said, glancing out at the pouring rain, "I do."

"Why is that?" she asked, knowing this was no innocent joke.

"I know that I want something from you."

"What?" she queried, stiffening her chin and firming her back. She knew the next words he'd say would be like taking a physical hit. She prepared herself. This was an all-too-familiar request. She knew a remark like that would only lead to trouble. Men had wanted something from her all her adult life. She often wondered if she had the words *use me* written on her forehead. From her first love in high school who copied every homework assignment from her and nearly got her expelled—to her ex-fiancé, a chef in his own right, who six years ago left her at the altar and stole her journal, which contained every recipe she'd created and claimed they were his. They all wanted something.

"I'm right-handed and the cut is on my right forefinger." He held up his hand. The tip of his finger was bloodred. "Do you think you could loosen the bandage before the tip of my finger pops off?" he said. She smiled, and then laughed out loud. "You know, I'm a bit concerned that seeing my soon-to-be gangrene finger, hand and arm amuses you."

She continued laughing. "I'm sorry, hold on." She hurried back to the sink, grabbed another Band-Aid, came back and this time put it on more gingerly.

"Thank you," he said. "You know when I was young my mother used to kiss me and make me feel better," he said playfully.

"Really," she said.

He nodded. "Yes, really," he spoke softly.

"Did it work for you? Did you feel better?"

His smile was pure seduction. "Immeasurably."

She leaned in close. He leaned down to her. She could see the anticipation in his eyes. "Then perhaps you should call your mother," she whispered.

He laughed out loud then stepped back and continued chuckling. When he finally stopped he looked at her and smiled. "You're different than I expected."

"What exactly did you expect?"

"I'm not really sure, just different."

In the sudden silence, she heard that the rain had started easing up. She should go. But it was difficult when his eyes were so focused on her. The seriousness of his expression unnerved her. She took a step back and he smiled. Did he know he was affecting her?

"Good night. Take care of that cut," she said, then turned to leave. But she didn't get far. Chase had grabbed and held her wrist. She turned as he pulled her into his arms. Her body slammed against his and a tiny gasp escaped. An instant later his mouth came down onto hers, taking her breath away. With her lips already parted from the gasp, he slipped his tongue into her mouth. He tasted like pure heaven.

She heard a sated groan of satisfaction rumble from his throat as if he'd been waiting to do this all evening. Her senses instantly scrambled. Her body responded of its own volition. Her heart raced, her stomach clenched and her nerve endings twitched and tingled. She felt her body give as he wrapped his arms around her and pressed her back between the door frame and his firm, hard body. She tilted her head and wrapped her arms around his neck. The kiss deepened even more. His tongue seduced her, and she met his demand with equal fervor.

This wasn't just a kiss. It had long since changed into something more primal and needful. It was raw passion gone wild. She moved her hips into his, feeling his emerging erection, and he pressed his into her. The motion became a tug-and-pull of bump and grind passion. Apparently, you didn't have to lie down and remove your clothes to make love. They were doing it with their tongues and mouths right there in the mud-room of her brother's home.

Then some semblance of sanity swept over her. If she didn't pull back now there was only one place this was going—right here on the floor in front of the washer and dryer. It seemed they both came to the same imminent conclusion because he pulled back at the exact same time she did. A split second passed. She opened her eyes. He looked just as surprised as she was. They were both breathing hard.

"Oh, my God, what am I doing?"

"This," he said, and began to pull her into his arms again.

"No, wait. Are you married, engaged?"

"No, of course not. Do you think I would have kissed you if I were married or engaged to someone?"

Nikita didn't know what to think. She only knew one thing. "I gotta go. Good night."

Chase watched Nikita turn and run across the driveway to her car. She got in and seconds later drove away. He watched the red lights until they disappeared around the corner, then closed the door and walked back into the kitchen, smiling. It wasn't the initial meeting he'd planned, but it certainly was memorable.

He touched his lips. "Damn, that was good," he said aloud, licking his lips and tasting her one more time. "Tasty." He walked over to the refrigerator, opened the door and looked inside. She'd left two complete left-over meals for him along with directions on how to re-heat them.

He frowned. Doing his job would mean taking her on. He was up for the challenge, and after this evening was sure she was, too. He just regretted that she'd lose.

Chapter 4

Three days passed and the weekend came. Saturday morning, Nikita busied herself with the usual pre-café opening duties. She got in at four-thirty in the morning, prepared dough and baked the first round of assorted pastries, sweet breads, desserts and mouthwatering delights. Afterward, she visited the produce and seafood markets returning with ingredients for the afternoon's lunch specialty. Later, after the bustling lunch crowd had dissipated and the café closed, the kitchen staff took a lunch break while having their weekly meeting. Nikita made final changes to the next week's work schedule and addressed any necessary concerns from the past week.

When the meeting was over the staff cleaned up and prepared to leave for the day. Darcy checked the kitchen while Nikita headed to the storeroom and pantry. The last thing to do each day was to take and confirm inventory for the coming week.

When Darcy was finished, she came to the storeroom doorway. "Hey, you ready for me?" Nikita asked when she saw her there.

"Yep, whenever you are," Darcy said, holding her cell phone and a computer pad. "Okay, tonight's catering job is all set. Rented tables, linens, flowers and buffet essentials are already on site for final prep. And all the buffet dishes are already headed to the Teen Dream Center's kitchen. We have to finalize plans for next week's catering job and confirm your schedule for the private chef gig I just landed for you. You wanted one or two more, but I think this one alone is gonna do it. The money is awesome. He basically agreed to my first number, which was totally insane, didn't even bother to haggle the price with me. I love when that happens."

"Private chef, huh?" Nikita asked as she continued counting and cross-checking inventory numbers.

"Yep, his office called and asked for you to start as early as this coming week. He really wants you."

She sighed loudly. "How long's the job?"

"Two weeks, maybe three with the possibility of extending."

Nikita thought about her last private chef job. The family of five on vacation in Key West, three children and a mother and father, were all insanely picky eaters who were constantly late and off schedule and they complained about everything. It lasted for three weeks. They were a constant pain but the money was well worth it. "How does it look on the schedule?"

"No real problems. You'll have to sync up after your cooking class at the Teen Dream Center on Tuesdays and Thursdays. But, and I quote, 'his schedule is flexible and will conform to whatever your needs are.' That's a direct quote as per his assistant."

Nikita stopped writing down the inventory numbers, turned and looked at Darcy. "Who is this client?"

"Apparently you made a lasting impression. It's Chase Buchanan."

"Chase Buchanan," she repeated as her nerves shuddered.

"Yep, he's been coming in and eating at the café for the last few days. He apparently loves the food. But if you ask me, he was more than just eating here. He was up to something. Then this afternoon his assistant called with the request."

A quiver of heat instantly shot through her body as her stomach clenched. This was no lasting impression. She reached up and touched her lips. The kiss was days ago, but the vivid memory of them pinned against the door frame wrapped in each other's arms continued. "Tell me about him."

"He's sexy, stunning, rich, intelligent…"

"No. About his personal life. Is he married, engaged, seeing someone?"

"Now how would I know that?"

"You know everything," Nikita said.

Darcy smiled. "Yeah, true that. Okay, I hear he's not married or engaged. He's not seeing anyone seriously as far as I've learned and he dates all the time—mostly first dates only. I think he might have commitment issues. The women are usually the professional or glamorous types, you know, lawyers, models, heiresses and an actress or two. Now tell me why you want to know. Are you interested in him?"

Nikita exhaled slowly. "I just wanted to know the types of food he might want me to cook. You know menu planning for a single man is different than for a dating or committed man." Darcy nodded her understanding. It made sense, but Nikita still couldn't believe she was actually able to pull that off so quickly. "Did you accept yet?"

"No, of course not," Darcy said, frowning, "you know I always confirm private gigs with you before offering the client a contract. His assistant called with an interest, I gave him our basic fee and guidelines and he accepted everything without dispute. I wish we had more potential clients like him."

Nikita shook her head. "Let me think about it." She wrote down the last inventory numbers, then went back to the office. "I'll get back to you with my answer tomorrow afternoon."

"Sure." Darcy followed her. "You know, you've been off the past few days. What's going on with you?"

"What?" Nikita looked up from her desk. "Nothing. Everything's fine. I'm fine," she said.

"Come on. I know you better than that. We go back a few hundred years, remember. I tell you about a dream job and all you can say is you'll think about it. No, I don't buy it. Something's up."

"Darcy, really, I'm fine."

Darcy eyed Nikita closely as she sat at the desk inputting the inventory numbers. "Maybe you're just working too hard. You're nonstop from four o'clock in the morning until late at night. The schedule has got to be taking its toll on you. You look terrible."

"Thanks," Nikita said sarcastically.

"You know what I mean," Darcy defended. "You look exhausted, like you haven't slept in days. Are you sure you want to do this job tonight? You can still pass. I'll call Leroy in to supervise the buffet table and waiters. It's a benefit, so our services are free and we're buying half the buffet table food as an added donation."

"I'm fine, just a little tired. I haven't been sleeping well, but I'm definitely going tonight. It's a Teen Dream Center benefit and I have to be there. Natalia and Mia will strangle me if I don't go." Nikita looked at her watch. It was three o'clock. "You know what, I'm gonna go home and take a short nap then get over to the center around five." She grabbed her backpack and everything she'd need for the catering job.

Darcy grabbed her purse and headed to the door, as well. "I'll see you later," she said.

"Okay, see you at the center," Nikita said, getting into her car.

She drove home on automatic pilot while thinking about all the things she had to do in the next few days. Then she remembered her new job. She was hesitant about accepting it. Darcy said the money was good, and Nikita certainly needed that, but to accept the job she knew she'd have to meet with Chase and discuss his plans. Then she'd spend two to three weeks cooking for him. That could be dangerous. He got to her, no question about it. She still couldn't believe she allowed that to happen. Five more minutes in his arms and she would have been flat on her back.

Her imagination took wing after that. She started thinking about all the things they could have done had the rain continued to pour down. On the floor, against the wall, on the washing machine... The imagery continued. Her stomach quivered. "No, just stop thinking about him," she chastised herself as she pulled into the garage and parked.

She grabbed the newspaper and mail from the front porch, went inside then headed straight up to her bedroom. She collapsed down in the big comfortable chair by the front window and looked out. Darcy was right, she was working too hard. But getting the money to extend her café was her dream. She closed her eyes, happily thinking about everything she wanted. Moments later her stomach quivered. She knew exactly what it was. It was him. He was in the back of her thoughts again.

She pulled out her cell phone, set her alarm and picked up the newspaper to flip through. The last thing she wanted to think about was Chase Buchanan. Then the first thing she saw was a photo of him on the front page of the *Key West Citizen*. He was smiling, posed and shaking hands with a couple of businessmen and the mayor. She folded the newspaper and tossed it aside. "Enough," she said aloud to the empty room. She'd just made her decision. She was not going to accept the private chef job. Satisfied with her resolution, she closed her eyes, expecting to just still her thoughts and rest. Instead, she slept.

Just like the dreams she'd been having the past few nights, this one was just as sexually arousing. In the dream she kept telling herself it wasn't real, so it didn't matter what happened or what she did. She slowly opened her eyes. She was outside in a field walking toward a house she didn't recognize. It started raining and she ran for cover. What she had thought was a house was actually an old barn. Wet from the rain, she stood in the open doors, waiting. Moments later, she realized she wasn't alone. She tensed as a familiar voice whispered to her. "Relax. Let go."

Firm, strong hands came up her arms to massage her shoulders, rub her neck and caress her back. She closed her eyes and drifted on the sensual stimulation he aroused in her. He gently guided her back, to lean flush against his body. Tender nibbling kisses trailed down her neck and across her shoulders. She raised her arms and wrapped them around his neck, holding him tight. His hands came up to cover her breasts. She arched her back, feeling the tingling touch of his palms tantalizing her hardened nipples. He pinched and rolled them between his fingers and thumbs, sending a torturous burn of pleasure to her core. The mind-blowing sensation was tearing her apart.

"Do you want more?" he whispered as his hands traveled down her stomach to dip between her legs.

She gasped and opened her eyes breathlessly and looked around. She was in her bedroom. And her phone was ringing. She answered, then realized it wasn't the cell phone ringing. It was the alarm she'd set earlier. She turned it off and eased back into the comfortable chair, looking up at the ceiling and thinking about her dream. She remembered everything. No need to analyze it; it was obvious. She knew what it was about. She wanted Chase. But every fiber in her being warned her to stay away. So she'd pass on the job and keep her distance. He'd eventually finish whatever business he was here to do, then go back to wherever he was from and she'd get back to her life. She nodded. It was a plan.

She glanced at her cell phone to check the time. It was getting late and she needed to shower and get dressed. The day wasn't over yet.

Chapter 5

He had slipped. It was an unparalleled blunder, and he didn't do blunders. Chase stared at the computer monitor, still thinking about what had happened three days ago. He couldn't get it out of his mind any more than he could get her out. Nikita was indelibly ingrained and he didn't like it. When she mentioned that she had a date, he was about to say that he didn't realize she was dating anyone. That would have been a mistake. There was no way he could say that without her questioning his foreknowledge of her personal life. He caught himself in time, but it never should have happened. He got careless and slipped, letting emotion out.

But what really troubled him was that he was bothered by the comment. More precisely, he was jealous. However minute or fleeting, the jealous feeling he had was still there. He didn't do jealous. She was his job, but after just one meeting and interaction, she was much more and that wasn't working for him.

The past few days he had stopped by the café hoping to see her. When he asked one of the waitresses about her, she told him that Nikita seldom came out of the kitchen during the day, except for when her sisters came in. So, short of stalking the place 24/7, he decided to step up his game. He donated a large sum of money to her sister Natalia's program, Teen Dream Center. That got him an invite to the benefit. He knew she'd attend.

He glanced around Mikhail Coles's home office. It certainly was impressive, even rivaling his home office in London. He wasn't sure how Andre knew Mikhail, but it was most opportune. He had needed a place to work, and Mikhail was out of town. But he'd be back at the end of the month. But more important, the project Chase needed to complete had an even more pressing deadline. One he could not miss.

He was a closer by profession. He got things done and finished jobs others couldn't. He was creative and used every weapon in his arsenal to get what his company needed. If Titan needed it done, he did it. His official title was Vice President of International Research. He traveled the world buying property and connecting with local officials to ease the way for Titan to come in. But he had ethics. Anything illegal was out of the question. He didn't bribe or coerce, but he did manipulate.

He thought about Nikita and wondered what it would take to get to her. He had some ideas. A slow, easy smile pulled at his mouth. One was particularly pleasurable.

But as he'd learned quickly, she was no fool. He'd have to open himself to her to get her to trust him.

He looked at his watch. It was time. He closed the laptop, stood up, grabbed his jacket and headed to the front door. He glanced at himself in the mirror as he walked through the foyer. Nothing had physically changed in the few days he'd been here in Key West. He was the same man. Still, all of a sudden he didn't feel the same. Maybe Daniel was right. This wasn't the job for him. There was something about Nikita Coles that was opening him up and he couldn't chance that. He needed to focus on the job. The sooner he got what he came for, the sooner he'd be back where he belonged—safe and away from her.

He got in his car and drove, following the GPS directions to the Teen Dream Center. As he walked in he was greeted by two stunning women standing at the door. "Good evening and welcome to the Teen Dream benefit. My name is Natalia Coles-Montgomery and this is my associate, Mia Morales."

"Ms. Coles-Montgomery, Ms. Morales," he began, knowing who they were, of course, and to whom they were each married. He knew just about everything there was to know about the Coles family. Natalia was married to movie star David Montgomery and Mia Morales was married to Stephen Morales, Natalia's cousin. Mia was several months pregnant. She had a very noticeable bump. "Ladies, it's a pleasure to be here. Thank you for the invitation. My name is Chase Buchanan."

Mia smiled brightly. "Yes, of course, Mr. Buchanan. It's a pleasure to meet you. I spoke with you on the phone yesterday. Nat, this is the huge contributor I told you about."

"I hope the check arrived okay," Chase said.

"Yes, it came by special messenger just a few minutes after we spoke," Mia replied.

Natalia shook his hand. "Mr. Buchanan, it's a pleasure to meet you. Mia told me to expect you this evening. Thank you so much for the very generous contribution to the center."

"You're very welcome. I've already contacted my company for a matching contribution, so you should hear from them soon," he said as he watched the two women look at each other, obviously overjoyed.

"Thank you," they said in unison.

"My pleasure." He glanced around quickly. "I spent a great deal of my teen years in a place similar to this. My mom was a single mother and she worked constantly. Places like this saved my life and even though the center I attended has long since closed, it's my privilege to give back whenever I can."

The women's faces lit up with pride and exhilaration. "That's very kind of you."

He looked around again. "It looks like quite a celebration."

"It is. Please go in and enjoy yourself. My sister Nikita Coles of Nikita's Café prepared an amazing buffet and my brother-in-law, Spencer Cage, will be performing later this evening."

"Spencer Cage. I'm a big fan."

"Well, I'll make sure you're introduced," Natalia promised.

"Sounds wonderful," he said, nodding. "Thank you." He continued inside as the two women greeted a couple walking in behind him.

At first glance the place seemed small, but as he walked around he realized it was much larger than he first assumed. He walked down the hall past the offices and a few classroomlike rooms, and then came to a more open area. The celebration was taking place in the great hall, which he assumed also served as the auditorium and play area. He walked through the double doors into a large open space. He was greeted again by several teens dressed in their best clothing excitedly chatting about the evening's events. Spencer Cage was top on the conversation list.

There were easily a couple hundred people already there mingling, talking, laughing and enjoying themselves. He looked around, seeing a few faces he recognized. He nodded in greeting to several people, then headed across the room to the buffet tables.

"Chase Buchanan."

Chase turned around to see city commissioner and local businessman and Realtor Oren Davis smiling generously as he hurried up beside him. The man could be his own cartoon character—floppy ash-blond hair, perpetual spray-on tan, round, stout, barrel-like physique and an abundance of perfectly white, expensive teeth.

"I thought that was you," Oren proclaimed as the two men shook hands cordially.

"Mr. Davis, good evening. It's good to see you again."

"Oren. Call me Oren, please. We're practically neighbors." Chase looked confused as Oren clarified. "You're staying at the Coleses' home on the hill. Beautiful home. I have to say, I had no idea you knew Mikhail Coles."

"I don't. The company rented the home for my convenience," Chase said, neglecting to relay that his brother, Andre, knew Mikhail well.

"Ah, I see. Well, pity I didn't know you'd be attending this event tonight. Damn nice program we have here. I'm glad I came up with the idea and put it together. It helps a lot of kiddies, you see, and that's what I'm all about— helping, giving back." He looked around, prideful.

"Wait, *you* came up with this program?" Chase asked, knowing of course that he hadn't. "Excuse me but I was under impression that this was the brainchild of Natalia Coles-Montgomery, and that she and her cousin, Mia Morales, ran it together. I didn't see your name on any of the literature."

"Well, technically, they are related and worked to relay my ideas in a more determined path of recognition. Low-key, under the radar, if you know what I mean," he blustered completely incoherently while winking knowingly.

Chase tired to keep his poker face, but Oren was really testing it. "Actually, Oren, I don't quite know what you mean."

"Essentially it was more like I was thinking about the program, if you know what I mean. I had it in my head for a while, mulling it over and letting it marinate but then it was already here. So, in essence, I did indeed have the initial idea and program for this wonderful event and evening, if you know what I mean."

"I'm still not sure I do," Chase said.

"No matter, it's a wonderful evening, and had I known you were coming, I would have brought my beautiful daughter and suggested the wife and I swing by and pick you up."

"Not necessary. My evening suddenly opened up and I decided to attend at the last minute."

"I'm glad you're here. Saves me having to call you tomorrow."

"Oh, is there business we need to discuss?" Chase asked curiously.

"No, no—well, yes. Actually it's on a more personal nature."

"Personal, how so?" Chase asked.

"Are you alone?" Oren asked, looking around him cautiously.

"Yes."

"No, not just this evening. Are you here in Key West alone?"

Chase smiled. "I am."

"Excellent." He chuckled happily and leaned closer. "Few people know this, but I fancy myself a bit of a matchmaker. I've gotten husbands for three of my four daughters. As soon as I met you I thought of my daughter, Crystal.

"By chance I just happened to mention your name to her at the dinner table the other evening. Surprisingly, she knew exactly who you were. She's quite stunning you know. She and her sisters won just about every Little Miss Pageant there is and she was fourth runner-up to Miss Teen North America Beauty and Talent Pageant a few years back. She would have taken the crown if her sisters hadn't come in the top three categories.

"She's smart as a whip and very athletic, a real catch if you get my meaning," he said, winking. "At any rate, she is very interested in meeting you, and I think you'd enjoy meeting her, as well, if you get my meaning. And, quite frankly I might add, a more personal alliance between our two very prominent families would be extremely beneficial to both of us given your company's current interest in local property, if you get my meaning."

Chase was an excellent poker player. Showing no outward emotion and keeping his expression placid had always served him well. This time was no different. He allowed Davis to make his pitch knowing there was no way he was going along with this. "Mr. Davis…"

"Please, call me Oren," he repeated.

Chase nodded. "Oren, it's very kind of you to consider me, but I don't intend to be here long and I never mix business with pleasure."

"Are you certain about that?" Oren said in a more challenging tone. The nearly blinding white teeth came out again. "I can be very persuasive and very helpful, particularly in matters of certain property acquisitions."

Chase smiled, trying not to lose his composure, but Oren was definitely testing it. With every job there was inevitably an attempt to bribe, coerce or even threaten him with money, property or power. He never accepted anything, obviously. And not surprisingly, this wasn't the first time he'd been offered someone's daughter. But in his estimation, a businessman selling out his family would sell out anyone. "Sir, Titan's business stands as is. What I'm proposing to bring to the table is Titan, not myself. And, as I mentioned the other night at dinner, this is all on spec. There are other locations, some far more suitable. This is merely my first stop in a series of possible locations."

"But I understand you already purchased property in the area."

"Yes, but property can very easily be sold or held as an investment. Nothing in my business is set in stone until I say it is. If you get my meaning." He added Oren's nervous catchphrase.

"Yes, yes, of course. But Alaska is quite a distance from our little patch of land here in Key West." He chuckled more nervously this time with a definite tenseness behind it. "I just don't want you to feel left out or lonely here in our fair city. My daughter is very familiar with everything Key West. She could be a great benefit to you and Titan while you're here. Walk into any location with her on your arm and doors will open."

"I thank you for your consideration, but I must show no level of bias. You understand of course."

"Yes, yes, of course. But you might just change your mind when I tell you that she has the biggest—"

"Mr. Buchanan." Both men turned to the beautiful woman who addressed him. Chase smiled immediately. "Good evening, Oren. Nice to see you. Gentlemen, please excuse my interruption. I'm Tatiana Cage. My sister, Natalia, mentioned that you'd like to meet my husband, Spencer Cage."

Chase smiled, delighted by the interruption. "Yes,

I would indeed. I told your sister that I'm a big fan," he said, then turned to Oren. "Oren, please excuse us a moment."

"Yes, yes, of course," Oren said.

Chase and Tatiana walked off, then a few feet away she began to slow her pace and then she stopped and turned to him. "Mr. Buchanan, I must apologize. I lied to you."

Chase looked at her. "Oh?"

"My husband hasn't arrived yet. I passed by a moment ago and just happened to overhear a bit of your conversation with Oren. You're new here in town and that puts a very definite target on your back."

"What kind of target?" Chase asked.

"Key West is a small community so when a single man of obvious means comes to town, he's fair game. And I don't mean Monopoly. I thought you might need…"

"Rescuing?" Chase offered.

Tatiana nodded. "I hope I haven't overstepped."

He chuckled. "No, not at all, your timing was perfect, and the interruption was most definitely appreciated. Thank you."

"You're very welcome," she said as they laughed. Tatiana's cell phone beeped. "Excuse me," she said as she glanced at it, quickly reading the text message. "Well, it looks like I didn't lie after all. My husband just arrived. I'll find him and introduce you. In the meantime, why don't you help yourself to the buffet? Nick has prepared an incredible spread."

"Nick?" Chase questioned.

"Nikita, my other sister. I believe you've already met."

Chase looked at her intensely as he nodded. He knew the three Coles sisters were very close but she showed no sign of knowing about the kiss he and Nikita shared a few days ago. "Yes, of course," he said. "She catered a dinner at your brother's home for me. She's a very talented chef. Is she here this evening? I'd like to thank her again for the other night."

"Yes, she's here somewhere," Tatiana said, looking around. "Umm, let's see. Ah, there she is coming out of the kitchen over by the buffet table." Her cell phone beeped again. "Excuse me." She looked at the text message and then began texting back.

Chase followed her line of vision and saw Nikita as she entered the room. She was laughing. Her associate, Darcy, was right behind her. He smiled. Seeing Nikita changed everything. She took his breath away. She had on a dark blue dress with thin straps and a deep neckline. It wasn't tight, but it did ease and flow seductively against each luscious curve of her body. She was stunning. Beside him, Tatiana was talking about the program, but he wasn't paying attention to what she was saying. All he saw was Nikita. She was bright and happy and completely unguarded. It was the perfect time to connect with her again.

"I'm sorry, Mr. Buchanan, I have to run backstage. The program is about to begin. Enjoy. I'll make sure to introduce you to Spencer after the show."

"No problem. I'll see you after the program," Chase said, finally tearing his eyes away from Nikita's face.

He spared a quick glance at Tatiana as she walked away. Then he noticed Oren Davis was smiling with those teeth and nodding at him. He nodded back then turned to where Nikita had been a moment ago. She was gone. He walked over and waited a few minutes, looking around casually as he prepared a small plate of hors d'oeuvres. He spoke briefly with those around him as he ate and waited for her to come back out.

But she didn't return.

Chapter 6

The program began. Nikita stayed in the back of the room by the buffet table, watching her sister shine. Natalia was a natural at the podium even though she insisted she hated speaking in public. Her speech was brilliant. She was funny and insightful all while extending the center's gratitude and prompting for more donations. When she finished, Nikita applauded long and loud, smiling with pride and delight.

Her oldest brother, Dominik, and cousin, Stephen, walked over and each hugged her. "Don't try to be nice to me," she whispered. "You're both late and you know I'm going to tell on you."

"Not my fault. I had to deliver twins," Dominik said as he grabbed a plate and began piling on food.

Stephen held his hands up in surrender. "I just got

off work. To protect and serve, remember. So what'd we miss?" he asked, following Dominik to the buffet table.

"Just the whole beginning of Nat's speech, that's all," she chastised jokingly, "so you know she's gonna strangle you both."

"Not if you don't tell her we were late," Dominik said.

Nikita chuckled ominously.

"Ah, come on, Niki, we'll make it worth your while," Stephen promised. Dominik agreed.

"Don't try to bribe me," she said. Dominik and Stephen looked at each other and chuckled. Nikita joined in as they all knew she wouldn't tell. They stood in silence as Natalia continued talking. Then they applauded when Mia joined her on the small stage.

Nikita glanced at Stephen. His eyes shone and sparkled at seeing his wife and her baby bump. The love and pride in his eyes was heartwarming. Nikita was touched and silently resolved that since she'd never see a man look at her that way, seeing others joyfully in love was all she needed.

Mia spoke a few minutes, then introduced the mayor. Next, the three would give out the teen awards.

Natalia's husband, David, and their sons came over. "Hey, when'd you guys get here?" he asked.

"Oh, a while ago," Stephen exaggerated. Dominik nodded in agreement, his mouth filled with food. Nikita shook her head.

"David, I thought the boys were in the nursery," she said.

"They were, but I promised them they could see their mom on stage."

"It looks like they're getting sleepy," she said.

"Yeah, they are." His cell phone beeped with a text message. He checked it out. "They need me backstage."

"Here, give them to me," Nikita said, taking one-year-old Jayden in her arms and three-and-a-half-year-old Brice's hand. "I'll take them back to the nursery."

They stayed a little while longer then Nikita and the boys left the room and headed down the hall and around the corner to the nursery. Since the center offered baby-sitting services, there were a number of children already there. Some grabbed nibbles from the kiddy buffet, others watched a movie and some were in the story-time center. Brice hurried over to the center to join some of his young friends. Jayden wanted to go, too, but she told him she'd read him a story. He settled down quickly then climbed into her arms.

Four pages into the six-page story he yawned and snuggled close. She wrapped her arms around him and continued reading. A few minutes later he was fast asleep. She laid him in one of the cribs, then checked on Brice. He was having the time of his life playing with a set of building toys. She sat down to help.

She smiled. Being with her nephews, even for such a short amount of time, warmed her heart. They were bright, gregarious and inquisitive. With her schedule as crazy as it was, she seldom got a chance to be with them, so when she did, she treasured their time together. It might sound cynical, but she knew they were the closest she'd ever get to being a mother.

Being left at the altar could do that to a person. Six years ago she stood and watched her fiancé jump into a cab with his best friend's sister and drive off. The signs were there; she'd just chosen to ignore them. Afterward, she was fine with it. The only thing that nagged at her was the why. He never said a word, he just left. No explanation. No justification. He just left her. It was the not knowing why that had left her emotionally paralyzed.

So, waiting for her life to begin had long since taken a toll on her. If she weren't so busy with her business she'd definitely do as her sister Natalia had done and go the in vitro fertilization route. Natalia's happily-ever-after ending was her two adorable boys. But now being an aunt was the most precious job Nikita could imagine. She got to spoil the boys relentlessly, free of any parental responsibility.

"Aunt Niki, look what I did," Brice said, hurrying over to her with a plane made out of building blocks.

Nikita smiled bright. "Ah, sweets, that's beautiful."

Brice frowned. "It's not beautiful. It's a plane. Planes can't be beautiful."

"Some planes can be beautiful," she said.

"No way," he said, shaking his head adamantly.

"How about planes with bright yellow flowers painted on them?"

Brice laughed. "No, planes don't have yellow flowers," he declared.

"You're right," she agreed. "Planes with bright yellow flowers and pink bananas. They're beautiful."

He laughed. "I'm gonna show Mommy and Daddy." He turned quickly. She grabbed his hand before he got away.

"Whoa, wait a minute. I have a better idea. We'll show Mommy and Daddy in a little bit, okay?"

"When's a little bit?"

She was just about to answer when a minibattle broke out on the other side of the room between two little boys who wanted the same toy. The two professional baby-sitters hurried over, but the crying and yelling woke Jayden. He started crying, too. Nikita hurried over to soothe him. Brice followed.

She began to pat and rub Jayden's back gently. A few moments later he drifted back to sleep. Nikita turned back to Brice. "Okay, little man, let me see that plane again." But Brice was gone.

Chase applauded as did everyone in the room. The evening's focus had shifted from a casual gathering to a more official evening of brief speeches, disbursement of awards and accolades. With everyone standing still he was able to get a better idea of his surroundings. The room was even more crowded than before. He stood to the side away from the main gathering by the small stage. He glanced around in full panoramic view, nodding to those he knew, such as the mayor and those women who made sure to be seen by him.

That's when he spotted her. She stood in the back with three men, one of whom he recognized as movie star David Montgomery. He held two young boys, then handed them off to her and walked away. She stood talking with the boys and the other two men for a few minutes. With focused determination he headed in that direction but was stopped short. Oren, who had apparently gotten his daughter there, stood directly in his path.

"Ah, here you are," Oren began excitedly. "Chase, this very lovely young lady is my daughter, Crystal. She came all the way here just to meet you."

Crystal smiled in her best pageant style without saying a word. Except for her thin, small frame, she was the spitting image of her father—long ash-blond hair, spray tan and large white teeth. Where his ample girth was around his middle, hers took the form of huge melonlike breasts that nearly popped out of her tiny low-cut dress.

"Good evening," he said, glancing away quickly and seeing Nikita and the young boys leave the room.

The conversation with Oren and Crystal was tedious and lasted much longer than he'd hoped. It was pretty much centered on Oren touting the joys of marriage and the readiness of his daughter to walk down the aisle. As he talked, she stood posed with her two very prominent assets brushing against his arm.

Unfortunately, Tatiana, his previous rescuer, was nowhere in sight. Still Oren talked, and Crystal stood smiling dutifully while her father relayed every one of her many accomplishments since sixth grade. Chase was polite, but his attention had long since been diverted. He excused himself soon after eleventh grade. Oren promised to continue at a later date. Chase walked out into the hall and looked around. Then he walked to the front entrance. He didn't see Nikita. He turned to go in the opposite direction farther into the center.

He walked down the hall and noticed a little boy who'd just turned the far corner and was walking toward him with some kind of toy in his hand. With definite purpose, he was headed to the main area near the front door. Chase frowned. The scene was completely wrong. There was no way a young child should have been out walking the halls alone. Chase saw the sign on the wall pointing to the nursery and presumed he'd walked out unnoticed. As the young boy got closer he recognized him to be the child Nikita had walked out with earlier.

"Hi," Chase said to the boy.

"No strangers," the little boy said pointedly and put his hand up to stop and block all conversation. Then he kept walking dismissively while looking straight ahead.

Chase chuckled. The little boy seemed more like a little man. "Yes, you're absolutely right. You did that very well. No strangers. But should you be out here all alone like this? I don't think that's a very good idea, do you?"

The little boy stopped and looked confused. He frowned, seeming to think hard about the question. "I have a plane to show Mommy and Daddy," he finally said.

"Wow, that's a cool-looking plane. Who made it?" Chase asked, kneeling down to the boy's eye level.

"I did."

"You did!" Chase said in exaggerated amazement. "You are very talented. That's the coolest plane I've ever seen."

"Yes, and it's not beautiful. It's cool," he said proudly.

"Oh, yes, it's definitely cool and not beautiful. You're a very smart young man. Do you think you can point me to the nursery?"

Brice turned and pointed in the direction from which he'd just come. "That's where Jayden and Aunt Niki are."

"Aunt Niki," Chase repeated.

He nodded his head and started to walk away.

"Wait, one more thing. Can you take me to Aunt Niki, please?"

The little boy frowned. Apparently, his mission to show his toy to his parents was interrupted again. "Okay," he said reluctantly.

"Thank you," Chase said.

"Brice!" Nikita called out in a near panic.

"We're here," Chase said, looking up when he heard Nikita's voice calling out from around the corner.

Nikita came running around the corner just as Chase stood up. She ran right into him. "Sorry," she said quickly, then seeing Brice she immediately dropped down to her knees. "Brice, you know you're never to leave the nursery alone. You know that," she scolded. He frowned, looking scared. She grabbed him and hugged him tight. He wrapped his little arms around her neck and held on as she picked him up to hug.

"Thank you so much. He just ran out of the—" Nikita stopped when she realized who he was. "You."

"Good evening," Chase said, smiling.

"Hi," she said breathlessly. "Mr. Buchanan, I'm surprised. I didn't realize you were here this evening."

"I got here a while ago and just happened to run into this young man with a very cool plane. He was kind enough to show me the way to the nursery."

"Thank you," she said sincerely, placing Brice back down.

"This is my nephew, Brice. He likes planes."

"I don't blame him. I like planes, too."

"Do you have a plane?" Brice asked Chase. "My daddy has a plane."

"Yes, I do have a plane. A real big-boy plane."

Seeing one of the sitters holding the door open, Brice hurried back to the nursery. Chase and Nikita followed more slowly. "Thanks again. He's fast. He got away from me. I turned my head for an instant and he was gone."

"He seems like a great kid."

She smiled proudly. "He is."

They stood in the doorway looking into the nursery window. Brice was with the small group of boys again. They were gathered together building what looked like a small metropolis. "So, here you are at the teen center," she began. "You really seem to get around."

"I like to keep busy when I'm traveling but tonight I thought I'd just enjoy a wonderful evening out." They turned and headed back to the program.

"May I ask you something?"

"Again," he said.

She nodded. "Yes, again."

"Sure."

"What exactly do you do, Mr. Buchanan?" she asked.

"I'm a structural engineer."

"Oh, is something falling down here in Key West?"

He chuckled. "No, I don't think so."

"Then what brings a structural engineer to our little corner of the world? And how does he come into town and arrange to meet with the mayor and city commission members almost instantly?"

"I'm very good at my job, and I enjoy meeting people."

"That's not an answer."

"Vacation," he offered, knowing she wouldn't believe him.

It was her turn to laugh. "Somehow I doubt that. I can't imagine a man like you taking vacations."

"I relax on occasion, like now."

"What is Titan Corporation doing here?" she asked again. "And I'm sure you can answer the question without divulging some top-secret plan of vital stock information."

"We're assessing investment property for future development."

Nikita's heart jumped. She knew when an oil company came in and bought property it wasn't just to plant flowers. She didn't know exactly what Titan was building, but she knew it was going to be major. "Do you intend to build an oil refinery here?"

"No. Definitely not."

"Then what?"

"I'm afraid I can't say right now."

"Okay, that's what Titan wants. Tell me this—what do *you* want here, Mr. Buchanan?" she asked.

He smiled. "First, I want you to call me Chase."

She nodded. "Okay, what do you want, Chase?"

"Is world peace too broad an answer?"

She smiled. "Yes."

He considered avoiding her questions again, but then decided to tell her the truth. "A large part of my job is troubleshooting problems. When there's a problem I go in and solve it."

"Is there a problem?"

"Yes."

"What kind of problem are you attempting to solve now?"

"Right now—this moment—you."

"Me," she said surprised. "How am I a problem?"

"You're very inquisitive. But, okay, to answer your question, right now my problem is that I'm standing here with a beautiful woman enjoying a great evening dedicated to a very worthy cause and all she's interesting in taking about is my business life. That's most definitely a problem."

She smiled, nodding. "You're good."

"Yes, I am, very good," he said seductively.

"So, Chase, what else are you good at?" She flirted openly.

He smiled. "Is that finally a question of interest?"

"Down boy. No, I'm just curious. Do you collect stamps, play checkers, scuba dive, salsa in the moonlight…?"

"I play chess. Perhaps we can play sometime after dinner."

"Are you asking me out to dinner, Chase?"

"Yes, I believe I am."

"Umm, look, you seem like a nice guy, and I don't want to lead you on or give you the wrong idea. What happened between us the other night was… It was just a kiss. It wasn't expected and certainly wasn't planned. It didn't mean anything and it wasn't an invitation to pursue me. I'm not looking for emotional intimacy or anything serious like that."

He smiled. "I understand."

"Good," she said, then turned to walk away.

"Now, may I ask you a question?" he asked.

She turned. "Sure."

"What *are* you looking for, Nikita?"

She opened her mouth, and then closed it quickly. She knew going in this direction was dangerous. She was already too attracted to him and temptation was pushing her right in his direction. "We're both rational and single adults with physical needs. There's obviously an attraction between us, so I suggest we satisfy our more carnal needs and dispense with the pretense of societal formality."

He laughed out loud. "Okay," he said slowly, then paused, considering what she had just suggested. Suddenly there was laughter coming from down the hall. They paused as a man and woman walked by, smiled and kept going.

"I'm looking for just sex," she said plainly.

"Just sex," he repeated.

"Yes, just sex. No commitments, no feelings or emotional attachments, just physical connection."

He nodded. "I can do just sex," he said. "And for the record, I asked you out for dinner, Nikita. I didn't ask you to marry me and have my children. That'll come later," he joked, and then winked.

She chuckled, amused by his genuine humor. "Funny."

"So, as they say, your place or mine?" he asked.

Chapter 7

Chase followed Nikita's red taillights through the city then out beyond the Key West Airport on Overseas Highway to Stock Island. She turned right at the second exit and drove down through the small community to the end of the peninsula. They continued down to an unpaved road. A few minutes later she pulled up beside a small A-frame beach cottage with a narrow wraparound porch surrounded by large mature palm trees. The house seemed to be in the middle of nowhere. He watched as she got out, walked to the back, and then leaned against the rear of her car, looking straight out into the night.

Chase parked beside her, then got out. Mirroring her actions, he leaned against the rear of his car.

"Nice car," she said, looking straight ahead.

He nodded. "Thanks."

"What kind is it, an Aston Martin?" she asked.

"No, it's a Fisker Karma. It's a plug-in hybrid. It gets great mileage and it's very good for the environment."

"Because of course Titan Energy Corporation is so concerned for the environment."

He smiled. "Exactly," he said, noting her obvious sarcasm. "You're not an environmentalist or I wouldn't be here. So what are you?"

"Curious," she said, glancing over to him.

"Curious is good." She looked away and they lapsed into a brief moment of silence. Chase looked up at the sky. The dark cloudless night hung heavy as the luminous moon shone down. A hot, sultry breeze swelled up around them as they stood side by side looking out into the silent night. It was quiet and serene. The taste of salt air laced his lips and the brackish smell of the ocean wafted gently in the air. He listened to the sound of waves crashing in the near distance. They were obviously close to the water. "It's nice here. Very still," he said breaking their easy silence.

She nodded. "Yes, it is. It's peaceful. I can usually only come here on the weekends."

"This isn't your home, is it?" he wondered aloud, turning to see her profile. Again, she stole his breath in the deep blue dress and strappy stiletto heels. Her hair was pulled up loosely and secured with a silver clip and she wore tiny diamond-stud earrings, two in each ear lobe along with a single dangle of diamonds. Her eyes were dusted with a glimmer of shadow, and the soft brush of color on her cheeks added to her natural blush. Her lips were gently touched with mauve lipstick, and the faint floral aroma of her delicate fragrance perfumed the air around her.

"No, it's not my main residence. I have a condo in the city, sixth floor, great view." She sighed peacefully and looked up at the millions of stars in the sky. "This is my hideaway. I think everybody needs something like this—a place to go where they can release."

With his eyes still hypnotically on her, he moved away from his car to stand right in front. She looked up at him with a seductive smile that nearly burned his insides to cinders. His arousal, which had started the moment he saw her three days before, was complete. Slowly, unhurriedly, he leaned down and kissed her lips tenderly, then he kissed and nibbled along her jaw and down her neck. "Tell me," he whispered close to her ear, "am I your release, Nikita?"

She closed her eyes. He was turning the simple act of kissing into a world-record event. Her mind clouded and she floated dizzily on each heart-stopping, knee-weakening, toe-curling nibble. He nuzzled closer still, sending a shock wave of hunger raging through her system. A burning heat flowed inside of her like lava down a mountainside, pooling in a pit of smoldering desire right between her legs. She took a deep breath and exhaled slowly, nodding absently. "You are tonight," she whispered.

"And what about tomorrow?" he questioned, leaning back to tip her chin up to meet his eyes. They stared eye to eye; neither flinched nor looked away. There was something there, something between them that was more than just desire. They both felt it.

"Tomorrow is a long way away," she said.

He leaned close—just inches from her parted lips. His chest brushed against her protruding nipples. She quivered inside. "So all you want is the physical," he said. She nodded. "Tonight and in the future," he clarified. She nodded again. "Then I guess we should make the best of what we have right now."

He kissed her hard, ravaging her mouth with more passion than she knew existed. It was insatiable. It was too much and not nearly enough. She wrapped her arms around his neck and he pulled her close, careful not to lean her back against the car. Intensity matched desire as their heads turned side to side, pressing deeper and deeper, devouring the rush of wanton need. When the kiss finally ended he dropped his mouth to her neck and nibbled gently, contrasting the ravaging kiss. Each tiny kiss made her stomach clench and quiver.

"You are such a bad idea for me," she muttered breathlessly.

He nodded. "Mmm-hmm, you're right, I am."

She bit at her lower lip as his mouth found hers again. The kiss exploded into a fusion of surging anticipation. Wild and unrestrained, they couldn't get enough. Then all of the sudden the fervent passion slowed to seductive teasing once again. He tenderly embraced the smooth curve of her neck, cradled the back of her head and dipped his forehead to hers. He waited a few moments, then he leaned back. "Maybe we should go inside."

She nodded. "Yeah, good idea," she said, taking his hand and leading him down the narrow path to the front door. She opened it and walked into complete darkness. She toggled the light switch, but nothing happened. "Hold on. The bulb must have blown out." Seconds later a light came on in the small living room. "Come on in," she said, "and have a seat. I'll be right back." She turned on the sound system as she walked by. Smooth jazz began playing instantly.

Chase walked into the small living room and looked around. It was the perfect beach cottage with distressed oak floors, scatter rugs and whitewashed walls with matching wainscoting. There were two large, white linen, overstuffed loveseats separated by an oblong coffee table topped with several cookbooks, one authored by Nikita Coles. He picked it up and thumbed through the pages.

It was a mixture of colorful food and table settings, photographs, recipes, party planning guides and anecdotal suggestions for avoiding kitchen disasters. He turned to the page with a photo of Nikita laughing with a man at her side. Chase recognized him instantly. He was her ex-fiancé, Reed Blackwell.

He knew the story. Nikita and Reed were engaged but he had apparently wanted to still play around. Reed walked out on her the day of their wedding, then returned five days later married to his best friend's sister and begged Nikita to take him back. She refused. When his family found out that he'd given Nikita land and this cottage as an engagement gift, they were furious and demanded it back. She refused and the courts all sided with her since she'd legally bought it from him for one dollar and a kiss. That same land was now worth millions and even more to Titan. Chase shook his head. "Hell hath no fury…"

"Hey, remember me?"

He turned, seeing Nikita standing in the archway holding a bottle of wine, a corkscrew and two glasses. The lights behind her made her glow in stunning brilliance. He smiled in pure admiration. She walked over to see what he was holding. He turned to the front cover. "Your cookbook looks pretty interesting," he said. "Where can I get a copy?"

"Unfortunately you can't. It's out of print now. But it did pretty well a few years ago. Wine?" she offered.

"Sure." He put the book back on the coffee table and took the bottle from her. She held the glasses as he opened it and poured, then placed the bottle down. She handed him his glass and he held it up to toast. "Here's to releases."

She smiled, toasted and sipped her wine, then sat down in one of the comfortable love seats. He sat beside her. "You're a very private man," she said. He nodded. "I have a feeling you know a lot more about me than you let on. But I don't know much about you."

"You didn't search me on the internet?" he questioned.

"Yeah, I did," she admitted freely. They both knew everyone searched Google for everyone. "But there's not a lot of personal information listed on you—only a lot of business stuff that seems to bring up more questions than they answer. For instance, it doesn't mention an ex-wife or an ex-fiancée, so I assume you've never been in a committed relationship." He nodded. "There was something that mentioned that you were in an accident recently."

"I was. My car hit some ice and I slid into a tree."

"Are you okay?"

He smiled and nodded. "Yes, I'm fine. It happened several months ago. What else do you want to know about me?"

"You have a slight accent. Where are you from originally?"

"I was born in Alaska. When I was two weeks old my mother moved to Europe for a new start. I've lived in France, Switzerland, England, Italy and a few other countries."

"So you're from all over. Where do you live now?"

"Mostly in Alaska, sometimes in France," he said evasively.

"How many languages do you speak?"

"Not as many as I should. English, French and Italian get you around Europe very easily if you don't go too far into the local dialect variations. There's also Hyōjungo Japanese, which can get you around most of the Far East, and Swahili, Berber and Yorùbá are a safe bet in Africa. *Êtes-vous impressionné?*"

"Oui, très," she answered in French without even thinking. Then she smiled and a brief moment of awareness passed between them. They were connecting and it felt comfortable.

"I like your home. It's very inviting. I assume the coast isn't too far away."

She nodded. "Actually it's a few blocks away. This area is built up on a higher level because of storm surges.

For some reason it makes it sound as if the waves are just outside the front door. Would you like to see the rest of the house?"

"Sure."

She held her glass and took him to the small, connected dining room, and then to her kitchen. It was, of course, immaculate and filled with every imaginable appliance and cooking convenience, as well as being by far the largest room in the house. There was also a small kitchen nook to the side with a stained-glass bay window, comfortable cushions and a large selection of cookbooks on the surrounding bookshelves. "That's a nice touch," he said, "I really like this area. It looks comfortable and cozy."

"It's one of my favorite places."

He looked at her. "I bet this is where you create your recipes, right?"

"Sometimes, but I have another much larger alcove in…" She paused a few seconds, then continued, "My bedroom."

"Oh," he said. The one word seemed to mean a thousand others.

She continued the tour then, taking him back to the front foyer then up the stairs to the second floor. There was a narrow hallway with three closed doors. She opened the closest one and walked in. He followed. She flipped a switch and soft lighting illuminated her bedroom. She went straight to the center of the room, then turned to him. "And this is my bedroom," she announced needlessly.

Nikita watched as he walked around, nodding approvingly. She tried to see the space for the first time as he did. Her bedroom was one huge area that encompassed most of the top level. She'd had a wall knocked out between two of the three bedrooms to increase the size of the master bedroom suite. The room was efficiently divided into a small office area with a desk, cabinets and a lounge chair, and a bedroom area with a queen-size bed. Then there was the alcove area, which as its large size would attest was more like a second sleeping area.

Chase walked over, sat down in the alcove and looked at her. His smile was pure pleasure. "Come here," he barely whispered.

She walked over to stand right in front of him. She leaned down and kissed him tenderly. *"Alors, vous voulez à faire amour ce soir?"*

He smiled. *"Oui. Sì. Ja. Sim. Nidiyo. Yebo. Hai. Shi. Da."*

She laughed at his extended answer. "Okay, okay, I get it. I think I can take that for a yes."

"Oh, that's very definitely a yes," he said.

"Good." She set her glass down and took his hand. He stood and followed her as she guided him to the bed and sat him down. She helped him remove his jacket and then loosened and pulled his tie free. She unbuttoned his shirt and pulled it from his pants. His chest was bare and his muscles were tight and well defined. She smiled seeing him. He was magnificent. She touched him and he jerked slightly. "Ticklish?"

He shook his head. "Aroused."

She nodded, then went over to the nightstand, opened the top drawer and pulled out a condom.

He leaned back and watched her. "Only one?" he queried.

She turned and smiled, then pulled out one more. He chuckled, got up and walked over to the nightstand and stood right behind her. He reached in and pulled out two more. She instantly felt his erection press against her. Her stomach quivered. He was definitely hard and ready.

She turned into his embrace. Having Chase here with her gave her several delicious ideas. She touched his bare chest, pushing him to sit down on the side of the bed again. She turned around so he could unzip her dress. She let it fall to the floor, then stepped out and faced him. Standing in her blue lace panties and matching strapless bra, she looked down at him. He licked his lips staring in admiration. She smiled. This was exactly what she wanted to see, the perfect reaction.

He reached up and ran two fingers over the sweet swell of her budding breasts. He licked his lips again, then let his hands drift down to her waist and around back to her rear. He held, cradled, massaged and then caressed each cheek, feeling their perky roundness. He squeezed gently then released her. He looked up into her hooded eyes. "Do you have any idea how much I want you right now?"

She knelt down on the bed, straddling him. The hardness between his legs stuck out at her instantly. "Yeah, I think I have a pretty good idea."

They were now face-to-face, eye to eye and mouth to mouth. She reached up between them and unsnapped her bra. Her breasts bounced free, her nipples pointed directly at him. He dipped his head down to lick the tip of her nipple. She gasped and quivered. When he licked the other, her body jerked back and her stomach quaked, but he held her in place. An instant later he captured her in a mouthful of torturous pleasure. His masterful tongue tantalized her as his lips and mouth devoured her. She held tight to his shoulders as her mind shattered into a million pieces.

He wrapped his arms around her and pulled her close. The quick action stole her breath away. An instant later he kissed her with explosive power. They were consumed as the swell of passion surged to abandoned bliss. He laid her down beside him and quickly removed his pants and underwear. Then his hand came down between her legs and through her lace panties began stroking and massaging her. She was wet and it seemed to excite him even more. "You're wet. You feel so good," he muttered in her ear as he nibbled her neck and his fingers toyed with her true pleasure. Her hips began to gyrate of their own volition. This wasn't what she expected, but right now all she knew was that she needed his hand right where it was.

Then he stopped, leaned back to look down the length of her nearly naked body. Her breasts peaked like twin mountaintops with nipples hard as cut diamonds. She reached down to feel him. He was hard, thick and long. Her stomach quivered. It had been a long time for her and he was so big. She leaned up and pressed her hand on his chest. He rolled onto his back with ease. She grabbed the condom package, opened it and slowly rolled it down his erection. She stroked and teased, knowing it was torturing him to remain still, but he did.

When he was well fitted, she climbed on top of him and kissed him. His hands came up to her with his thumbs circling her nipples. She moaned. Every nerve ending in her body felt as if it were about to explode. The kiss ended, and he began nibbling her neck, shoulder and chest. Then his mouth came to her breast. He took her in, suckling and savoring her bountiful flesh. He assailed the other, until her body arched and her legs trembled.

She pushed back and sat up, feeling his erection right at the entrance of her core. Then slowly, she eased down, filling herself, taking all of him. She felt every throbbing inch inside as her muscles clamped tightly around him. He groaned and held her waist. She began to move up and down, rolling and grinding her hips into him. Her breathing quickened to short gasps.

Her heart sped to match the pace she'd set. In, out, in, out, she surged over and over again. Rocking and riding him harder and harder. She panted, craving every inch of him inside of her again and again. Then she leaned back to sit tall and rock lower and deeper. He covered her bouncing breasts with his large hands that tantalized each nipple relentlessly.

The fury of passion raged as their climax approached. She held back as long as she could but she knew it was a losing battle. The first release escaped in a full spasm, making her scream his name. Her legs shook and she gasped a whimper but continued to ride him. He grabbed her hips tightly and began pounding upward, thrashing into her full force. He was coming and she was coming again. Their bodies tensed and tightened and shook as their release exploded. He slowed to deliberately measured, punctuated thrusts as his essence poured out. They tensed one last time, holding tight as ecstasy took them once more, and then slowly released them.

She opened her eyes. He was staring up at her with a smile that made her want to do it all over again.

"Hey, you okay?" he asked breathlessly.

She nodded and moved to get off, but he stopped her and pulled her down on top of his chest. Their breathing quickly synced as one. She closed her eyes again and enjoyed the feel of his long, gentle strokes on her back and down to her rear, the solidness of his chest and the treasure of him still inside of her.

She must have drifted to sleep because when she awoke she was lying on her stomach and he was right beside her, stroking and rubbing the length of her naked body. "Hey," she said lazily.

"Hi," he replied. "You have the most desirable body I have ever seen. And your rear is simply spectacular," he said, kissing each buttock to make his point.

"I bet you say that to all the women you know."

"No. I don't," he said with more sincerity than she expected.

She rolled over to face him. She was smiling. "You are so bad for me." She bit at her lower lip, then reached over to grab another condom from the nightstand. "Here, put this on," she said.

Already hard, he did. "Nice and slow this time," she told him.

He smiled. "Yes, ma'am, nice and slow."

They made love just as she asked—torturously slow and so very, very nice. Her on top, him on top, it didn't matter. In the end, their passion erupted into another mind-numbing climax—then another and another.

Chapter 8

Hours later Chase woke up to the beginning of daylight and squinted against the open drapes. He sat up and looked around. He was alone. Smiling, he remembered the night before. Nikita Coles was a remarkable woman and together they had been insatiable. They'd used three of the four condoms he'd pulled out and right now he was ready to use the fourth one.

The first time she had climbed on top and took charge and he liked it. There was no pretense of purpose or false timidity. She was bold and assertive and knew exactly what she wanted from him. She was tight, but the fit was still perfect. Lying here thinking about her, he could feel his body getting hard all over again.

He got up and went into the bathroom. There was everything he needed on the counter. He brushed his teeth, jumped in the shower, wrapped a towel around his hips and then went downstairs. The heavenly aroma drew him like a moth to an open flame. Nikita was in her chrome-and-marble sanctuary. She was sitting in the alcove beneath the large stained-glass bay window writing something in a book. He watched her a few moments, undetected.

She wore glasses and had her hair parted in the middle and braided on either side like schoolgirl. She had on an apron tied around her waist over a simple floor-length sundress. He didn't know what was more mouth-wateringly stimulating, the sight of her or the aroma of whatever was cooking in the oven.

"Good morning," he said, interrupting her. She looked up, smiling, and removed her glasses. He was still naked except for the towel wrapped and tied at his hips.

"Good morning. Your clothes are in the dryer."

"Thanks." He walked over to her, took the pen and notebook from her hands and pulled her to stand. Barefoot, she was much shorter. He untied the bowed apron and tossed it on the cushions, then looked down the length of her body. His towel poked out slightly in front as he pulled her into his arms and began kissing her.

"Mmm," she moaned between passionate kisses. "Oh, I have something in the oven."

"Me, too," he joked.

She giggled and pushed away. She went to the oven and pulled out two perfectly baked miniature cakes. The aroma was insane. She set the cake pans on the wired racks then turned and put another two small pans of batter in the oven.

"When are they coming out?" he rasped seductively.

"In about thirty to thirty-five minutes," she said.

"Perfect." He took her hand and led her to the front stairs. They climbed the first few steps and just before she got to the lower landing he stopped her. She turned to him. He was a step below. He wrapped his arms around waist and leaned up to kiss her. As the kiss deepened he began unbuttoning the four buttons at the front of her sundress. Her breasts, full, plump and inviting, peeked out. He dropped the next step down with his mouth open and devoured her instantly.

She held on to his shoulders and arched her back, giving him exactly what he wanted. Kissing, licking and sucking, his mouth was everywhere. She stood weakened by his amorous assault. "I can't wait. I need you now. Right now."

At her words he quickly pulled her dress and his towel away. They stood naked.

He kissed down the length of her body, then up again stopping at her stomach, waist and hips. He reached behind, caressed and massaged her rear, drawing her closer. "Mmm," he groaned deep and throaty, "suddenly I think I have an appetite."

"Okay, I can cook some eggs, bacon, pancakes and—"

"Nikita," he interrupted and looked up at her smiling. "Not that kind of appetite," he said softly.

"Oh?" she began as he pulled her to sit down on the step in front of him. "Oh." She realized exactly what he meant. He spread her legs, putting each on his shoulders, and she lay back on the landing. He lifted her rear off the step and with tender, relentless greed, licking and savoring, he ate his fill and more.

"Oh!" Nikita climaxed hard with an orgasm that was damn near blinding. Waves of rapturous spasms rippled through her. "Oh…"

He ripped the condom open and barely fitted himself before he entered her in one smooth fluid motion. They never made it upstairs to the bed.

Hours later Chase sat watching as Nikita picked herbs from her large backyard garden. Earlier, after making love on the steps, they had eaten breakfast, cleaned the kitchen and iced the tiny cakes. Then they walked around the extensive perimeter of her property. Now with a wicker basket over her arm and dressed in another floor-length sundress, this one more fitted to her body, Nikita walked down another makeshift aisle.

Each section was squared off with long wooden planks resembling open boxes—some with covered netting and some without. Like a playful butterfly she picked and chose her targets with selective ingenuity— first touching, smelling and examining and either passing them by or picking and storing them in her basket. Chase decided that he could watch her playful ritual all day.

But he was no fool. He knew Nikita would be upset when she found out what he wanted from her. He also knew she might assume their sleeping together was all part of his ruse to get what he wanted. The thing was he wasn't sure it wasn't.

Truth in fact, she was right. He had intended to get

closer to her and find her weakness and exploit it for Titan's gain. But unlike Daniel, he didn't want to come into Key West and start taking over. He needed the community and the prominent Coles family as allies if Titan was going to stay. Nikita was the key to everything.

He watched her bend down, gather a large handful of spiked greenery, and then pull it up from the earth. She brought the bunch up to her nose and inhaled. She smiled with overwhelming pleasure, as if she'd just breathed in the scent of a dozen roses. He half smiled, seeing her repeat the action over and over again.

He looked up. The sky was overcast. Still, it was easy to discern that it was nearly midday. It was Sunday and he knew he still had to work. He didn't even want to see his cell phone and email messages. He looked back at the garden. Nikita wasn't there. He scanned more closely and finally spotted her crouched low behind a high, colorful bush. She stood up and happily continued to the next section.

It was the simplest action and still it seemed to give her pure pleasure. Having obviously filled her basket to capacity and apparently very satisfied with her pickings, she walked back toward the house—toward him. "You looked like you were having fun out there," he said.

She smiled brightly. "I was. I love playing in my little garden." She turned, looking back admiringly. "Every year it seems to get smaller and smaller."

"How many acres do you have?" he asked.

She sat down next to him with her basket beside her. "Two, but most of it is just undeveloped grounds. The soil is too sandy to expand the garden. Still…"

"What you have is well-tended. Who waters and takes care of it when you're away all week?"

"Believe it or not there's a programmed and timed irrigation system that I can control wirelessly with my computer. I come and pick weeds when I can. Also, the Petersons, my housekeeper and her husband come in and help out a few times a week. They live on a fixed income and have an apartment a few miles away. They come here to putter in the garden and pick whatever they like. We're like growing partners. I supply the land and they tend it and take what they need. Last year they asked if some of their friends might help out, as well."

"So this plot of land helps others, too."

"More like we help each other," she said.

"Sounds like you have your corner of the world all worked out."

"Nah, not even close," she confessed, then showed obvious concern. "Coming here sometimes makes me sad. This used to be a thriving community about seventy years ago. As soon as I saw this area I loved it."

"And Reed gave it to you for a kiss."

She nodded. "In lieu of an engagement ring, he signed the deed over to me. It had been in his family for decades. His parents gave it to him and he gave it to me. Of course when they found out, they were furious. They demanded it back and even took me to court a few times. But it was a legally binding transaction. The cottage and land are mine."

"And you kept it after everything that happened."

"I've been offered a lot of money for it."

"Take the money."

She stopped and looked around. "This area will come back to life someday and when it does I'm going to build a restaurant here."

They slipped into a comfortable silence for a few moments, then she asked him, "You said last night that your mother moved to Europe to get a new start, but you didn't mention your father. Are they divorced?"

"My parents were never married. For the first fifteen years of my life my father had no idea I even existed," he admitted freely, something he never did. Few knew of his humble beginnings. "My father's family didn't accept their relationship so my father broke it off. He had no idea my mother was pregnant at the time."

"Wow," she muttered softly. "That must have been difficult for her and for you. Did you know about him?"

"No, not for a long while."

"So how did he eventually find out about you and vice versa?"

"My mother owned a small eatery outside of Paris. A magazine did an article on her. My grandfather, Jacob Buchanan, was in France at the time and he happened to see a picture of my mother and me in the magazine.

"He came to the café. He immediately recognized Mom and that I was a Buchanan. The next day he contacted her and demanded to meet me. She refused. This went on for months. As a Buchanan he tried everything, threats, money, but it was his promise to tell me everything that did it.

"After that she told me about my birth, about Titan, the Buchanans and my father. Jacob and Daniel came to meet me. They insisted on taking me back to Alaska to raise me, as they put it, the right way." He chuckled. "The rest is history."

"The right way. What's the right way?" she asked.

"The only way, the Buchanan way," he said.

"Did you go?"

"No. I didn't know them. All I knew at the time was my home in Paris. I stubbornly refused, also a Buchanan way, apparently."

"I guess everything worked out in the end."

"Yeah, something like that. My mother was killed in an accident and I went to live in Alaska. My grandparents raised me."

"And what about your father?" she asked.

"I preferred to stay with my grandparents, Olivia and Jacob. My father objected but..."

"Let me guess. You stubbornly refused."

"Exactly."

She looked at him. "Demanded, huh?"

He smiled and nodded. "You'd have to know my family to get it. The Buchanans rule the world. Whatever they want, they get—period. They have money and power in abundance. That's tempting and very seductive to a lot of people. Few adamantly turn it down. Eventually everyone surrenders to them. In the end, they always win."

"*Them* and *they* are you," she said simply, identifying the truth in his statement.

"Yes, I am a Buchanan," he said with a mixture of pride, arrogance and disdain. He shot her a look, his eyes intense and piercing, that seemed to warn her off. "Never forget that," he spoke softly.

She nodded. Then, as if a cool chill shivered down her spine, she stood abruptly. "Are you ready to go?" she asked, grabbing her basket.

He nodded, took the basket and set it beside him on the top step. He pulled her in between his long legs and gathered her in his arms. He held her tight, kissing and nuzzling her neck tenderly. Making love with her was so natural. He could see himself doing it for the rest of his life.

He kissed her lips long and leisurely. When the kiss ended he leaned back. For a moment he didn't speak. He just enjoyed the feel of her, knowing this would probably be the end of them. After all, this was exactly what it was. Not a love thing, not a relationship thing, but a sex thing and now it was time to let it go.

"Thank you for bringing me here. It's beautiful. You're beautiful," he said.

She nodded. "Come on." She took his hand and led him back to the house.

After dropping off one of the small cakes to the Petersons, they headed back to the city, him in his car and her in hers. When they crossed into the Key West city limits she glanced up in the rearview mirror. Chase beeped his horn and turned in the direction of her brother's home. It was time to get back to her real life. She drove through town to the beachfront area and her sister's home.

As soon as she got out of the car she heard the laughter and squeals of her two nephews coming from the back of the house. She walked down the side path and reached over to open the gate. A flash of bright colors dashed by in the distance then disappeared, followed by another flash of color. Nikita knew it was her nephews.

They appeared again. This time she stepped back and rang the chimes and bells at the gate's entrance. Two tiny cuties stopped and turned instantly to see who it was. They were dressed as superheroes in swimming trunks, goggles and towels for capes. They were flying around the backyard. Nikita rang the bells again. Their faces lit up and they came running. Nikita couldn't help but laugh. They held their arms out and flew to her. She leaned down and grabbed them in one fell swoop.

Nearly knocking her over and toppling the small cake boxes in her hand, the three laughed as Natalia came to see who it was. "Hey," Natalia said, waving. "Come on back."

Nikita laughed as the boys realized she was holding two cake boxes. "Ooh! What's that? Is that a cake? Is that for us? Is that for us?" they excitedly repeated over and over again.

"Only if your mother says it's okay. So you'll have to ask…"

They immediately ran off to their mother before she even finished the sentence. By the time Nikita reached her sister, the boys were jumping up and down excitedly. "She said yes!" they cheered.

Natalia told the boys to calm down, put on their T-shirts, wash their hands and go sit down at the kitchen table. When they ran off, she hugged Nikita warmly.

"You look great this morning," Nikita said.

"Thanks. I think I'm finally getting over the cold that

never came. I've been feeling so run-down and tired lately, but today I feel great."

"Maybe it was the Teen Center event," Nikita said.

"Yeah, probably. David made me promise to see a doctor if I didn't get any better."

"Actually, that's a good idea. I agree with him. You should do it. I'll watch the boys."

"But—hey—check you out, girl. Your face is practically glowing. What have you been up to?"

"Me? Nothing, just working," Nikita said, then quickly changed the subject. "Last night was fantastic, Nat. Everything was wonderful. You and Mia did an amazing job."

Natalia nodded. "Thank you. Yes, it was great. The kids were so happy to be there and celebrate with us. We raised a lot of money for the scholarship fund and I'm so pleased. The teens worked so hard, and to be able to hand over a check to help them further their education is an amazing feeling. And thank you for everything you did. The catering and food were spectacular. I didn't get a chance to eat last night, but everybody raved about the food. Thank you so much. We really appreciated it."

"Oh, you're very welcome. It was our pleasure to participate. I'm just glad everything worked out," Nikita said.

"It did, beautifully."

Nikita lifted up the cake boxes. "I brought this by today 'cause I figured you probably didn't get any last night. Guess I was right."

"Yep, you were. But don't you even try to kiss up to me after what happened last night."

Nikita looked confused. "What do you mean? What happened last night?" she asked.

"You know you're in trouble, don't you?" Natalia said as she opened the back door and walked into the kitchen. The boys were already seated at the table.

"Trouble, why? What did I do?" Nikita said anxiously as she put the cake boxes on the counter, then went over and gave each nephew a kiss on the forehead.

"Don't pretend all innocent like you don't know what you did. That's why you baked and brought over the cake. You knew you were wrong for disappearing on me last night."

Nikita visibly relaxed. "Oh, that," she said casually.

"Oh, that," Natalia repeated. She gave the boys a slice of cake each and they immediately dug in. Then the sisters went back outside to sit on the back deck. "So what happened to you? Where'd you go?"

"You know I have to get up early."

Natalia laughed, knowing her sister too well. "You didn't have to open the café this morning and you never go to bed early when you don't have to open the next day. Plus you even have tomorrow off. Darcy already told me," Natalia said. Nikita looked guilty. "You might as well just tell me. You know I'm gonna find out anyway."

Nikita paused a moment then shook her head. She knew her sister was right, she would find out eventually. "I went to Stock Island," she said. Natalia looked at her, knowing there was more. Nikita took a deep breath and exhaled slowly. "Chase Buchanan came with me."

Natalia smiled. "So that's what happened to him. Oren Davis kept asking for him all night. The man was just about losing his mind. So, he was with you. Interesting. So… And…" She prompted for more.

"And nothing," Nikita said. "Would you please stop trying to get me down the aisle? I can see it written all over your face."

Natalia laughed. "Did I say anything about marriage? All I said was, interesting."

"Yeah, but I know your 'interesting.' It means that you mentally already have your dress picked out for the wedding."

"Hey, stop trying to do my job. I'm the psychologist in the family," Natalia joked.

"Doesn't matter, I know you too well, Nat. Marriage doesn't interest me. Not anymore. I've done all that, the falling in love thing. Never again. To love is to open yourself up to pain."

"Not always, Nikita. Finding that someone special— for you to love—will change that."

"But I'm not looking for someone to love," Nikita said.

Natalia smiled. "And that's exactly when they come along."

"No, not this time."

Natalia gave her a reassuring pat on the arm. "So tell me, hanging out with Chase Buchanan, what's he really like?"

"I don't know, nice. He's a lot different than I expected."

"What did you expect, an ogre because he's in the oil business?"

"No, not exactly." She paused to consider then

shrugged. "I don't know, he's just different. He's sweet, funny and kind of tender. He told me a lot about himself and his family. I was surprised. He seemed to be the closed-off type, but he's not."

"It sounds like you two got to know each other a bit."

"We did. We talked and then got to know each other a lot more. We had sex. And before you get all romance-novel-happily-ever-after on me, it was just a physical release. We both needed it."

"A physical release," Natalia repeated.

Nikita nodded. "Exactly, a physical release—four times."

Natalia's mouth gaped open, then she chuckled. "Whoa, four times? Damn, girl, are you sure that it was just a physical release? Once, twice, maybe is no big deal physical. But when you get into four times in one night, you're talking serious attraction. Add in the talking, and that's two people getting to know one another real well. It sounds like it might be more than you think."

"Trust me, beyond the physical we have very little in common. He works for a huge oil company and the last time I checked, they nearly destroyed the Gulf and everything around it, including my café."

"That had nothing to do with Titan Energy and you know it."

"It doesn't matter. Oil companies have tried to stake a claim in this area before. I have a feeling he's here to do the same thing."

"Did he say that?"

"No, not exactly," Nikita said.

"Then you don't really know. Niki, maybe you're letting your experience with Reed's family influence your objectivity. Just because they're both in the oil business doesn't mean that Reed and Chase are alike. Reed's family came in with big plans and big promises to help this community. They wound up almost destroying it."

"And how do we know the Buchanans aren't going to do the exact same thing?"

"We don't know," Natalia said.

"No, we don't," Nikita confirmed, then paused for a moment.

"You know there's a book out about them, the Buchanans."

"Really," Nikita said then, shook her head. "It's probably just another hyped-up, self-promoting, tell-nothing book."

"No. Actually it's pretty good. It's about Jacob Buchanan and the Titan Energy Corporation and it's written by Johanna Butler before she became Andre Buchanan's wife."

"Then how objective can it possibly be?"

"All I know is that it's a good book. It tells the good and the bad of how their ancestor Thaddeus Boles became Louis Buchanan. It starts in New Orleans in 1863 and tells how they became the Buchanans of Alaska in the twenty-first century. Like I said, it's pretty good. Maybe you should check it out. You'd get a better insight into what Chase is all about."

"Maybe," Nikita said. Her sister was right, she didn't know what Chase and his family were up to, but she intended to find out. "Nat, I gotta go. Give David and the boys a kiss for me." She hugged her sister just as the boys called to her asking for more cake. "I'll catch up with you later."

As soon as she got into the car her cell phone rang. It was Darcy. She pressed the button on her steering wheel and answered. "Hey, what's up?"

"Everything's good. I just wanted to finalize this private chef job before tomorrow. Did you decide what you want to do about Chase Buchanan? I need to give them an answer as soon as possible."

"Um, yeah, I'm turning it down."

"For real—you're turning him down?" Darcy sounded surprised.

"Yes."

"Did I mention I gave them our top-tier fee?"

"Yes, and the answer is the same. I'm still turning them down."

"You know you're killing me, right?"

"You'll survive. I'll talk to you later." She ended the call and blasted her music all the way home.

Chapter 9

Chase ran along the beachfront path with the purpose and determination of an Olympic marathon contender a mile and a half behind the frontrunner. He was overdoing it, but he needed this. He was a man driven by both his desire and his need.

His desire was simple—it pulled him toward Nikita. But he needed to get his job done and the diversion with Nikita, once merely a means to an end, was suddenly more than he expected. Spending the night with Nikita was better than he ever imagined. She was remarkable—funny, smart, beautiful and just too damn sexy.

He'd played it close before by taking the more subtle route to his end result. To his credit, it had always worked. But that was before. Never had he allowed his feelings and emotions to go this deep. Nikita was doing this to him and he was letting her. She was getting him to open up. He needed to stop. He knew he needed to get close *to* her, without getting lost *in* her.

He still couldn't believe he'd told her things about himself, things no one knew about him or his family. She asked, he answered. It was impulse and it was stupid. He was losing his edge and passion was pushing him over.

He slowed his pace then eventually stopped running and looked around. The lush tropical scenery was breathtaking. He could definitely see himself living here. It wasn't that different from his home in France in the warmer months. He put his hands on his hips and took a few deep inhales to steady his breathing.

He started walking back toward the house knowing he had to continue what he started. Soon his walk became a jog and he was back to running again. He decided to take a shortcut back. A half mile from the house, he spotted a car coming toward him. The car suddenly slammed on its brakes and the driver window rolled down. "Chase. Chase."

It was Oren Davis. Chase nodded and waved then kept running.

Oren made an awkward U-turn, drove a bit, then pulled up beside him and stopped abruptly, calling to him again. "Chase, hold up."

Chase turned to see Oren waving as he got out of the car to catch up to him. He stopped running as Oren approached. "Hello, Oren," he said, catching his breath.

"Chase, how are you? I just stopped by the house. I guess I just missed you. I see you're out here exercising—fine day for a run. You know my daughter, Crystal, runs out here all the time. I'm surprised you haven't seen her. You can't miss her, she's so beautiful but, of course, you already know that," he said, then chuckled to himself.

"Listen, about that property you're trying to secure. I think I might have a possible solution. Why don't you stop by the house one evening this week for dinner and we'll flush out a few ideas."

"Actually, Oren, I'm going to be pretty busy the next few days. As I mentioned, Key West isn't the only area we're interested in pursuing."

"Yes. Yes, of course. I just thought that if you were interested we could get together and discuss a few other prime locations. That way we could—"

"Oren, I have to get back to the house. I'm expecting a very important phone call in a few minutes," he said, backing up.

"Oh, sure, of course, I was just going to mention that I can have Crystal stop by and—"

"Oren, I really have to go. I'll catch up with you later," Chase said, then crossed in front of Oren's car and continued running.

A few minutes later he walked into the house, stood in the large foyer and looked around with a satisfied smile on his face. He'd have to do something about Oren eventually. He shook his head and half chuckled as he headed upstairs to the master bedroom. He pulled out a pair of dark charcoal slacks and a gray cotton knit shirt, and then headed into the bathroom.

After a long hot, then cold shower he dried off, shaved and changed. He headed downstairs to the home office, and then sat down at the desk and opened his laptop.

The first thing he saw was that he had several messages since he'd checked earlier. Two were from Daniel. Neither of which he intended to answer anytime soon. He typed a message to his assistant and just as he hit the send key his cell phone rang. He checked out the caller ID, and then answered. "Hey."

"What's up, bro? How's it going down there in paradise?" Andre Buchanan said jokingly.

Hearing Andre's voice made him smile. Andre was nothing like their father. Where Daniel was abrasive and quick to act, Andre was calm, laid-back and level-headed. He was somewhere in the middle. "It's all good. I'm making headway. Where are you?" Chase asked.

"Alaska. Home."

"How's Johanna?"

"She's incredible."

Chase smiled. He could hear the broad smile in Andre's voice. "Dude, you know you really struck gold when she came into your life. I've never seen you happier. You're right, she's an incredible woman."

"She is," Andre agreed. "I don't know if you heard the news. I'm gonna be a father."

Chase chuckled. "For real? Excellent, that's fantastic news, Andre. Congratulations, I wish you and Johanna all the best. You'll be great parents."

"Man, I never thought I could be so happy."

"You know we have to celebrate when you get here," Chase said.

"For sure, sounds good. So, I hear Daniel's on your case. He wants the setup ASAP."

"Yeah, and that's an understatement. But what he

wants and what's gonna actually happen are two different things. He can't just come in and bulldoze the place. I told him that an aggressive takeover isn't what's needed in this case."

"You're preaching to the choir. I echoed that assessment six weeks ago. After the Gulf spill and the Blackwell deal debacle, there's no way the local community is just going to open their arms and welcome us. We have to tread lightly. I don't envy your position right now."

"I'm handling it okay. Getting me into Mikhail's house was a smart move. It puts me right in the center of everything. How well do you know the Coles family?"

"I know Mikhail. We go back a few years. I've met his brother, Dominik, who's a doctor at the local hospital, and I've worked with their sister, Tatiana. She's a journalist. She did a story on Titan a year and a half ago. She's very professional, fair and very good at her job. She just married Spencer Cage, the media mogul."

"Yeah. And her sister, Natalia, is married to David Montgomery."

"Yep, that's right."

"Interesting. What do you know about the other sister, Nikita?"

"I've never met her. She owns a bakery and café in town. I've had the food. She's good, very good. Have you talked to her yet?"

"Yes," Chase said without elaborating further.

"Is she willing to sell?"

"We haven't actually discussed it yet, but the local Realtor says no. I intend to find out why, eliminate the obstruction and then hopefully get her cooperation."

KIMANI
ROMANCE

An Important Message from the Publisher

Dear Reader,

Because you've chosen to read one of our fine novels, I'd like to say "thank you"! And, as a special way to say thank you, I'm offering to send you two more Kimani™ Romance novels and two surprise gifts— absolutely FREE! These books will keep it real with true-to-life African American characters that turn up the heat and sizzle with passion.

Please enjoy the free books and gifts with our compliments...

Glenda Howard
For Kimani Press™

Peel off Seal and Place Inside...

W e'd like to send you two free books to introduce you to Kimani™ Romance books. These novels feature strong, sexy women, and African-American heroes that are charming, loving and true. Our authors fill each page with exceptional dialogue, exciting plot twists, and enough sizzling romance to keep you riveted until the very end!

KIMANI ROMANCE...LOVE'S ULTIMATE DESTINATION

THE EDITOR'S "THANK YOU" FREE GIFTS INCLUDE:

> Two Kimani™ Romance Novels
> Two exciting surprise gifts

YES! I have placed my Editor's "thank you" Free Gifts seal in the space provided at right. Please send me 2 FREE Books, and my 2 FREE Mystery Gifts. I understand that I am under no obligation to purchase anything further, as explained on the back of this card.

PLACE FREE GIFTS SEAL HERE

168/368 XDL FTF5

Please Print

FIRST NAME

LAST NAME

ADDRESS

APT.#

CITY

STATE/PROV.

ZIP/POSTAL CODE

Thank You!

Offer limited to one per household and not applicable to series that subscriber is currently receiving.

The Reader Service - Here's How It Works:

"Psychology?"

"Whatever works," Chase said, "but she doesn't open up much."

"If anyone can get her to open up and sell, you can. So listen, I'm on my way to New York tomorrow then I'll swing down there at the end of the week. You gonna be around?"

"Yeah, I should be here."

"When's your meeting with the Federal Energy Regulatory Commission?"

"It's early next Monday. I don't foresee any problems."

"I agree. I have a few documents I want you to look over before you go. I think you'll find them helpful."

"Okay," Chase said.

"All right, I'll see you in a few days."

"Have a safe trip. See you later," Chase said, then disconnected the call. As soon as he did he saw that he had another email from Daniel and also one from Darcy Richardson at Nikita's Café. He opened and read the latter.

Five minutes later he was in his car and headed back into town.

After the short visit with her sister and a quick stop at home, Nikita drove into town. She parked, ran a few errands, then walked into the café. Business was bustling as usual. She spoke to a few regular customers, waved to the Sunday-afternoon counter staff, then continued to the kitchen. The sweet aroma of sugar and cinnamon dusted the air as Leroy placed a tray of elephant ear pastries on the baking rack to cool. The caramelized brown crisps, tinted top and bottom, smelled divine and looked just perfect.

"Hey," Darcy said, "what are you doing here? I finally get you two days off in a row and this is what you do, come in here? Hello, Nikita, it's your day off. Go home, relax."

"Yeah, yeah, I know. I am. I just need to grab a few recipes from the office," she said as she headed in that direction.

Darcy followed. "Listen, I know you said you wanted to turn the Chase job down, but are you sure?"

"Yeah, I'm very sure," Nikita said, sitting at her desk and opening her laptop. She began scanning her recipe files.

Darcy, standing in the doorway, leaned to the side and cocked her head, wondering. "Did something happen last night?"

Nikita look up at her quickly, anxiously. "What do you mean?"

"I mean yesterday you didn't seem this positive and now you're damn near adamant about not taking the job. I just thought maybe something happened to prompt this total certainty."

"Nothing happened. I thought about it and it's best if I pass."

Darcy shook her head. "I don't get it. This is the perfect job. One person, occasional guests, no drama—in and out, no big deal, just cook and leave. He seems easy enough to please."

Nikita smirked, knowing that was exactly the problem. She shook her head more from the heated memories of the night before then from anything Darcy had just said. "I have too much on my plate right now."

"You're forgetting I'm the one who makes your plate. If you really wanted this job, you could do it. We both know that. Or is there something else I need to know?"

"No, there's nothing else you need to know. Just thank him and drop it, okay?"

"Okay, sure, if you say so. I'll send the email right now."

"Good. Thanks. I'll be here for a little while."

"Okay," Darcy said, sounding suspicious, "I'll be up front."

Two hours later there was a knock on her office door. Nikita looked up, seeing Chase standing in the doorway smiling. "Good afternoon, Nikita," he said.

"Chase, hi, what are you doing here?" she asked, surprised.

"You refused me," he said, "so I came to find out why."

"I don't understand. Why what?" she asked, still too stunned seeing him standing in her office doorway.

"I got an email from your assistant. You refused my offer."

"Oh, right, that private chef thing. I can't. Sorry, I'm just too busy at the moment to take anything else on."

"No, you're not," he said, smirking knowingly as he began walking around her office looking at the many cookbooks, awards and certificates. "At least be honest with yourself."

"Excuse me," she said, leaning back and crossing her arms in front. Her defenses shot up instantly.

He turned back to her, still smiling. "You heard me. Yeah, you're busy, but at least admit the *real* truth. We both know."

"Which is?" she asked, then saw Leroy walk by the open door, Russ followed a few seconds later. Both men glanced in. Nikita walked over and closed the door then came back to her desk. She stood, leaning back casually.

"You're scared to do it," he said simply.

Her eyes narrowed. These were fighting words as far as she was concerned. He was challenging her and she didn't like it. "Scared of a Buchanan?" she said, chuckling. "I don't think so."

"Of me," he more than firmly clarified.

"Women don't say no to you often, do they?"

"No, not often," he admitted freely.

"Perhaps you should get used to it once in a while. Call this a one-off, and accept it. The answer is still no."

The seductive smile that appeared on his face told her exactly what he was thinking. His eyes drifted down the long length of her body, then back up to her face. He shook his head. "I'll triple the fee from your last job."

She immediately knew something was up. No one paid the money he was offering just to have her cook a few meals. He wanted something else from her and she knew exactly what it was. "Don't get confused because we slept together last night. It was physical pleasure, that's all. Remember, one time only."

"Actually, it was four times, but who's counting?"

"I'm not looking for anything from you. And if you're

looking for some kind of *Pretty Woman* scenario to play out while you're here, you've got the wrong woman. That's not my job description."

"To clarify my intentions—I'm looking for someone to prepare my meals. I will be entertaining business associates over the next few weeks. I don't want to worry about menus, preparations, schedules or whether or not everything is top quality. I want the best. I want you." His tone was all business, showing the true professional he was. "And as to your other point—our time together was great. No—correction—it was fantastic. But I can separate my personal life from my professional goal. The question is, can you?"

She nodded, metaphorically stepping up to the offer with equal professionalism. "Fine, I'll do it. Two weeks, right?" she asked.

"Three," he corrected, challenging her again.

"Fine, three weeks. Starting...?"

"Tomorrow night," he said instantly.

"Just you, right?"

"Tomorrow, yes, but there will be an occasional guest or two. You'll know in advance."

She nodded. "Darcy will handle the contract stipulations and your dietary details."

"Thank you."

"You're welcome." She grabbed her backpack and computer pad, opened her office door and left. When she got outside she stopped, realizing she'd just stormed out of her own office leaving him there. Good Lord, what was she thinking? But it was too late. Going back in would make her look like a nutcase. She got into her car and headed home. At the first traffic light she glanced in the rearview mirror. Chase was standing in front of her café smiling. She shook her head. This was crazy. She was crazy. He'd challenged and goaded her and she'd buckled under almost instantly. Crap.

Chapter 10

Nikita opened her eyes and rolled over. Sleep was impossible again tonight. The words repeated over and over in her mind like a jumbled children's nursery rhyme. *Private chef for Chase Buchanan, dinners only, the countdown was on, just sixteen more.* It had started at twenty, but so far she managed to get in and be out, fulfilling her contractual duties without seeing or interacting with him. He had business associates dine in with him the past four nights. But she had a feeling that was more his doing than hers. She also knew that was going to end soon.

Her main contact was Kelvin, Chase's assistant. She left suggested menus each night and he emailed any corrections and instructions as to number of dinner guests and meal variations. It was working perfectly so far. So far....

She reached out, grabbed her cell phone off the side table and checked the time. She'd only been in bed an hour, but it seemed like longer. She kept thinking about Chase and their one night together. "Damn," she muttered softly to herself in the still darkness. One night, that's all it took for her to fall for him. And admittedly, she had. Never one to hide her feelings or pretend to anyone including herself, she knew exactly how she felt and she didn't like it.

He was only here for a short time, so any relationship, physical or otherwise, was at best short-term. Serious was out of the question. But then she didn't want serious anyway, right? "Right," she answered herself aloud.

Every rational bone in her body warned her off him, but emotionally she couldn't help herself. She wanted him, but she refused to give in. She was stronger than that.

She closed her eyes and smiled as the memories came to life. On the steps with a towel and a sundress... She replayed in her mind their last time together. Her stomach quivered even now.

It had been five days. It was time to let it go—let him go. She was always the first to tell her sister that sex was just a dopamine release. Caffeine and chocolate could do the same thing. It was simply human nature and a simple act for procreation and pleasure. She'd had her pleasure; now it was time to move on. She rolled back over, closed her eyes, took a couple of deep breaths, and then eventually dozed off to sleep.

Hours later, Nikita was charged with a burst of energy. She had successfully gotten memories of her night with Chase out of her mind. She had put them in their place and now it was time to refocus.

She prepped, cooked and baked, getting everything ready for a vigorous day at the café. In the late afternoon she grabbed the mail and went into her office.

The tediousness of running a business never got to her much. Thankfully, she had Darcy who thrived on doing the meticulous, more mundane chores. She paid bills, arranged delivery schedules, handled the front counter staff and customers, leaving Nikita to stay mostly in the kitchen doing exactly what she loved doing.

Always on schedule, Nikita knew she had fifteen minutes before she had to leave and get to the Teen Dream Center for her cooking demonstration and class. She plopped down in her chair and called her friend at the real-estate office to set up an appointment to see her soon-to-be property next door. Two minutes into the conversation she nearly dropped the phone.

"Gone?" Nikita said, blinking in confusion. She stopped going through the mail on her desk as the word echoed in her ears like church bells on a Sunday morning. It wasn't possible.

"Wait, what?" she said, unwilling to believe what she was hearing. Everything she'd planned to do was contingent on buying this property.

"No, there's gotta be a mistake. I'm talking about the property right next door to my bakery. I'm going to break out the walls and expand."

"I know, Nikita, and there's no mistake," Wendy Carter said.

"But I've been talking to you about it for the last six

months. It's been on the market for over three years. No one's even looked at it in all that time except for me. So it can't be gone."

"I'm sorry, Nikita. There was nothing I could do."

"What do you mean there was nothing you could do? No, you're gonna have to tell whoever leased it that the property has already been spoken for."

"You know I can't do that. And I didn't say it was leased. I said it was sold."

"Sold? It can't be."

"Nikita, believe me, I know what a sold property looks like. It was purchased a week ago from an overseas client, sight unseen. I heard that it was a cash transaction, so you know the client must be seriously wealthy."

"That's crazy. Who buys a commercial property sight unseen? What are they going to do with it?" Nikita asked, expecting her friend to tell her. There was a definite pause. "That wasn't a rhetorical question, Wendy. Who's the client?"

"You know I can't divulge that information, Nikita. And besides, it's not even my account. It's my boss's sale and you know how Oren is."

"I can't believe this. Okay, do me a favor. Can you see if this overseas client would be interested in leasing it to me?"

"Sure, that I can do."

"Thanks."

"Listen, Nikita, I'm sorry about all this. I had no idea any of this was happening until the papers hit my desk this morning. I've gotta go. I have a meeting in a few minutes. I'll see what I can do about leasing."

"Okay, I'll talk to you later." Nikita hung up the office phone and just stared straight ahead, unable to believe what had happened.

"This is crazy," she muttered, "this is…" She paused. The faint aroma of done, quickly on the way to being well done got her attention. She hurried out of her office, grabbed two pot holders on the way and then yanked the oven door open. A blast of burning heat enveloped her as she reached in. Her pastries were tinted the perfect brown indicating they were just done. A second later would have been too late. She placed the two trays on the metal counter, and then smiled in exhilaration. There was nothing like seeing perfection.

"People, please," Nikita said, "we need to focus here."

"Sorry, I got it," Leroy said, grabbing the trays.

The kitchen door to the front café opened and Darcy walked in with her usual unhurried self.

"Good Lord, wouldn't you know it, the most gorgeous man I've ever seen in my life just walked into the bakery and I look a hot mess." She fanned her face with an overnight express mail envelope then handed it to Nikita. "And wouldn't you know it, he's wearing a wedding band. Hey, what are you still doing here?"

"I know. I know. I'm on my way out now. What's this?" Nikita asked absently.

"It was just delivered. It's for you personally, not the café."

"What is it?"

"Darling, you have to pull the little tab and open it to find out."

Nikita ignored the obvious sarcastic remark. She

opened the envelope and pulled out a very legal-looking document. She scanned it quickly then tossed it onto her desk.

"Another offer," Darcy surmised, picking it up.

"Yeah, I swear the Blackwells' attorneys must have sent me a small forest's worth of useless legal paperwork by now."

"It must be nice to be so popular," Darcy said.

"What do you mean popular?" Nikita asked.

"Check it out. This paperwork isn't from Reed's family. It's from Oren Davis Realty."

"Oren Davis? What does he want?"

Darcy handed the papers back to her. "You, apparently," she said, "or I guess more specifically, he wants your cottage."

"My cottage," Nikita repeated.

"Yep, he's making you an offer. But since when does Oren want a cottage on Stock Island?"

Nikita shook her head. She assumed he was still representing the Blackwell family. She shook her head. "I can't think about that right now. I'm not selling and his drama is the last thing on my list."

"Listen, since you're still here, that gorgeous man out front would like a moment of your time."

"Who is it?" she asked with more anticipation in her voice than she intended.

Darcy shrugged. "Don't know. He's tall, dark and gorgeous, but he's wearing a wedding band. You know that's all I ever see."

Nikita peeked out the kitchen door into the main café area. She saw the man Darcy described, but didn't recognize him. And she didn't have time to find out who he was. She looked at her watch and headed the opposite direction to the back door. Darcy followed. "I don't have time right now. Tell him I'm already gone."

Darcy nodded as Nikita walked out the back door. "Have fun at the cooking class. And try to stay home tomorrow."

Nikita waved and hurried to her car. She was running late.

An hour and a half later she left the Teen Dream Center and made a quick stop at the café for a sampling tray of her delectable delights. While she was in the center, Chase had left a text message that he and his guest were going to be a few minutes late. She knew Chase was expecting a guest this evening, she just didn't know who it was. A tiny part of her hoped it wasn't a date. She wasn't sure how she'd feel about cooking for him and another woman.

She got to her brother's house and hurried through the back door into the kitchen. She'd prepped the evening's meal earlier that day and readied everything per his request. There was a four-pound prime rib roast in the oven, seasoned red new potatoes and asparagus spears. Everything was back on schedule.

She quickly prepared a garden salad and a small tray of appetizers. She pulled medium-well prime rib steak out of the oven, placed it on the counter with a foil tent, then let it sit and rest to distribute the natural juices back into the meat.

She looked around and smiled approvingly. With

everything under control for the moment, she unbuttoned her chef's jacket, sat on the stool at the center island, grabbed her cell phone and checked her messages. There was nothing majorly important so she texted each of her sisters. Thinking about what Natalia suggested, she pulled out her eReader. A few minutes later, she found, downloaded and began reading about the life of Jacob Buchanan and the Titan Energy Corporation by Johanna Butler.

Two chapters in she had to admit the book was just as Natalia said—very interesting. It was amazing to read how a teenager had the foresight to change his fate and alter the destiny of his entire family. Just as she started chapter three, the doorbell rang. She looked up. Chase had a front door key, so she assumed it was his guest. Curious, she headed to the foyer.

Through the heavily tinted sidelights, she saw Crystal Davis standing at the door. She was dressed in a silky summer dress with a V-neckline so severe it looked as if the dress were split in half. It was very obviously meant to show her abundant double-D implants. Nikita looked down at her own modest attire. She wore her chef's jacket over a pair of jeans, a simple cotton shirt and comfortable flats. She shook her head and opened the door.

Crystal Davis turned smiling, then seeing Nikita, her facial expression instantly changed.

Nikita nearly laughed at seeing the comical transformation from sexy to shocked. "Hello, Crystal," she said nicely.

Chapter 11

"Nikita, what are you doing here?"

"You mean what am I doing here in my brother's home?"

"Yes, I mean, no. I mean, Mikhail is out of town and Chase is staying here, right?"

"Yes, he is," Nikita said.

"So, why are you here?"

Nikita and Crystal had a long history of polite altercations, most centered on the men in her life. Having failed miserably at trying to get her brothers and cousins down the aisle, Crystal, with her father's assistance, set her sights on any wealthy man coming into the Key West area. It didn't matter if they were already in a relationship or not. At one time she'd set her sights on Reed Blackwell, even after he and Nikita had announced their engagement.

"Chase isn't here," Nikita said, then moved to close the door.

"Wait. I want to come in and wait for him."

"Is he expecting you?"

She paused a few seconds. "Yes, of course," she said. "We're dining at my house this evening. I'm cooking, not that it's any of your business," she added snidely.

Nikita knew she was lying, and she intended to call her on it, but just before she replied, Chase pulled up in front of the house. She noticed that someone was in the passenger's seat. Nikita stepped back, not sure she wanted to see who he was with. The driver's door opened and Chase got out, laughing. An instant later a second man got out, also laughing. She saw that it was the same man from the café earlier.

As he turned to the front door, Chase smiled. "Well, this is certainly a copious welcome home," he said.

"Indeed," his guest replied.

"Chase, hello," Crystal said immediately, then seductively walked over to him in her five-inch Manolo Blahnik strappy stiletto sandals. She wrapped her arm in his as if they'd known each other for years. "I was hoping you'd get here soon."

"Did we have an appointment?" he asked Crystal, then glanced up at Nikita.

Nikita relaxed back against the front door frame, obviously enjoying this too much.

"Yes, of course. My father sent me to pick you up. He said you'd be joining us for dinner this evening. I cooked."

Chase looked at his guest, and then at Nikita. "Crystal, there must have been a miscommunication or a misunderstanding. I have a guest for dinner this evening."

Crystal looked over to the attractive man standing by the car. She smiled politely. "I have plenty for the two of you. Your guest is certainly welcome to join us."

Crystal's comment was intended exactly as she'd said it and it had nothing to do with food. Chase glanced at his guest, who shook his head as he looked away then centered his attention on the cell phone in his hand. Nikita nearly chuckled aloud.

"Actually, we have business we need to discuss," Chase told Crystal.

"I don't mind a little business with dinner."

"Crystal, perhaps a rain check would be better."

"Sure, okay. I'll tell my father." It seemed to come out like a threat. "You have a good evening." She kissed his cheek, glanced at Nikita, and then sashayed over to her car and drove off.

Chase looked up at Nikita in the doorway. She nodded, turned, then went back into the house.

Back in the kitchen, she washed her hands, buttoned her jacket and prepared to serve dinner. She put the warmed hors d'oeuvres on the island and checked the prime rib. Just as she heated the pan to quickly sauté the blanched asparagus, the kitchen door opened. Chase walked in, followed by his guest.

"Good evening, Nikita."

She turned, smiling. "Good evening, gentlemen. There are hors d'oeuvres on the island. Please help yourselves or I can bring them out to you in the dining room."

"Not necessary. Here is good," Chase said.

"Okay, dinner will be served in fifteen minutes unless you'd like more time."

"No, fifteen minutes sounds perfect. Nikita, this is Andre Buchanan. Andre, Nikita Coles, Mikhail's sister."

Nikita smiled. "It's a pleasure meeting you, Mr. Buchanan."

"Please call me Andre, and actually, the pleasure is all mine. Mikhail has spoken about you often. He raves about your cooking. And the last time I was in Key West I actually had the opportunity to see you on the local morning show. Do you still do cooking demonstrations?"

"Yes, I do. I tape once a week."

"I must say I'm very much looking forward to this evening's meal."

She nodded. "Then I hope you'll enjoy it. This evening I've prepared a light garden salad, a herbaceous prime rib roast with Marsala-enhanced au jus, buttered red skin whipped potatoes and sautéed scallion and asparagus. For dessert I've prepared a tray of the café's specialty, delectable delights. Please help yourselves to hors d'oeuvres." She motion toward the tray of assorted edibles.

Chase and Andre each picked up hors d'oeuvres, then another and another.

"So, you're Nikita as in Nikita's Café in town?" Andre asked.

"Yes," she said, adding wine to the sauté pan.

"I stopped by earlier this afternoon," Andre continued as he ate another hors d'oeuvre. "I asked to meet you, but you had apparently just left."

"I teach a cooking class at the local teen center. I hope there wasn't a problem with your order."

"No, not at all—on the contrary. I wanted to know if you shipped your delectable delights across the country. I sampled a few the last time I was here and I know my wife would simply love them."

"I'm sure we can help you out with that," Nikita said as she removed the foil tent on the rib roast. She looked up, seeing Chase and Andre's reaction. Their eyes seemed to glaze over as they each stopped chewing and just started at the meat platter. It was the exactly the reaction she expected.

"That looks incredible," Chase said. "I think we'd better change the fifteen minutes to two."

Andre nodded. "I agree, and you can skip the garden salad."

"Sounds good. I'll set the table in the dining room," Nikita said.

"Why don't we eat here?" Chase suggested. Andre agreed, grabbing another hors d'oeuvre and popping it into his mouth.

"I'm sure the last thing you want to do is enjoy your meal here in the kitchen while I'm cleaning up for the evening."

"Easy solve, join us," Chase said.

"I assume you have business to discuss."

"Nothing that can't wait," Andre said. "Please join us."

Nikita consented, and set three place settings on the island. Chase grabbed glasses and Andre opened a bottle of red wine.

Then she pulled out a sharp knife from her professional case. Both men watched with admiration as she sliced the prime rib. The succulent meat, perfectly cooked and juicy, cut like a hot knife through melted butter. She plated the food then served the picture-perfect dishes.

"This looks… Wow," Andre said.

"Yeah, exactly," Chase added.

"Please, eat, don't wait for me."

They instantly dug in with enthusiastic gusto. Nikita made a small plate for herself and by the time she turned to sit she saw that Chase and Andre were just about done. She brought the potatoes, asparagus and prime rib to the island, family style. Chase had seconds and Andre had thirds.

When the entrée was finished Nikita presented a tray of small dessert cakes and served coffee. They laughed and talked throughout the meal, speaking mainly about her culinary skills and background and their favorite meals and recipes. Andre confessed to being the world's worst cook and Chase admitted to at one time toying with the idea of following his mother's footsteps and taking over the family eatery in France.

"Nikita, you outdid yourself. That meal was beyond delicious," Chase complimented.

Andre nodded. "I totally agree. It was the best meal I've ever eaten in my life and if you tell Johanna that, I'll deny it."

They laughed. "It was my pleasure. I'm glad you enjoyed it," she said as she placed the leftovers in glass containers and put them in the refrigerator. She began clearing the dishes, and Chase and Andre helped. "Thank you for your help. I can take it from here. I'm sure you have business to discuss."

"Actually, I do have a few calls to make," Andre said. "Nikita, thank you again for a mouthwatering meal. It was a true pleasure."

"You're very welcome."

Andre left the kitchen. Chase stayed and watched as she continued cleaning up. When the place was spotless and the dishwasher was started she turned to him, leaning back against the counter. "So tell me, why didn't you go into the family business?" she asked.

"I did."

"I mean with your mother," she clarified.

"I got a more interesting offer."

"Titan," she surmised. He nodded. "An offer you couldn't refuse," she added.

"An offer I didn't want to refuse."

"Are you happy with your decision?" she asked.

He nodded. "Yes."

"Good. Then that's all that matters, that you like what you do." She paused a moment. "I like Andre. I can see how he and my brother are good friends. They have the same temperament."

"You'd like the rest of my family, too."

"You think so, huh?"

He came around the counter and approached her. "Mmm-hmm, I do. And you'd like Alaska, as well. It's wild, untamed and unpredictable, but it's also quiet, refined and very urbane."

"Really," she said, swallowing hard as he stood right

in front of her. He leaned down and pressed his lips to her cheek then slowly drifted down to her neck. "Um, what are you doing?" she asked needlessly.

"Kissing you and telling you about Alaska," he whispered innocently as he started unbuttoning the front of her chef's jacket.

"The scenery is breathtaking and the open wilderness is stunning. At dawn the early-morning air is sweet and clean…" He reached in and began softly stroking the underside of her breasts as his thumbs tickled her nipples. "And at dusk it's exactly the same way. And then there are the mountains, the glaciers, the trees, the skies and the oceans, each more spectacular than the next."

"It sounds amazing."

"It is. You should come visit me."

She chuckled softly. "No thanks, I prefer warm weather."

"It's warm and it gets hot, too," he said.

"But I thought Alaska was cold and rainy most of the time."

"Don't worry, I'll keep you warm," he said, touching his tongue to her earlobe.

"For how long?" she asked on a shudder.

"For as long as you want me."

"That could be a long time."

He didn't respond. He leaned back and smiled. "I'm hungry. I just need one small taste."

The seductive glint in his eyes told her exactly what he was hungry for—her. He licked his lips and her stomach quivered like Jell-O sitting on a washing machine. Seconds later, he unsnapped her jeans. She closed her eyes, summoned all the inner strength she had and stilled his hands. "Chase, I have to go."

He stopped. "Are you sure?" he asked. His voice was already husky with desire and need.

"Yes, I need to go," she said. He nodded, stepped back and leaned against the counter beside her just as his cell phone vibrated on the counter. He saw the caller ID, but didn't answer. "You probably should get that," she said. "It might be important."

"It's not."

She moved away and began gathering her things. The last thing she grabbed was her eReader. She immediately thought about what she had been reading, the book on the Buchanans. She looked up at Chase. He was watching her. She smiled then as a deep, intense longing washed over her. Wanting him was too easy. Having him was feeling too right and the possibility of loving him was getting to be too real. "Good night, Chase," she said softly.

"Good night, Nikita," he said, then waited until she got close to the mudroom to speak. "You know you were right, this is going to be trouble."

She paused a moment then smiled and answered over her shoulder. "That's okay, I've never been afraid of a little trouble."

Chapter 12

The next six days flew by quickly. It was business as usual. Nikita focused on working at the café during the day, and then fulfilling her contract and preparing Chase's meals in the evening. They were usually something simple since he typically entertained business associates. They ate, she cleaned up, they talked business and she left. Her life was back to normal, but in the back of her mind there was a nagging thought that stayed with her. Chase Buchanan was a temptation she couldn't afford to satisfy again. One night with him had to be enough.

Nikita slept hard and long. She didn't have to go to work in the morning, so she didn't set her alarm and it felt good to just sleep in. She awoke around six-thirty, relaxed and energized. She opened her eyes and looked over at the morning's bright sunshine beaming through the sheer curtains. She already knew it was going to be a great day. She didn't have anything in particular planned. She relaxed back and closed her eyes again.

She didn't remember her dreams as she usually did, but she had a feeling Chase was there. He was always there. She dreamed about him almost nightly. Shaking the stray thoughts away, she got up, showered, dressed and then headed downstairs to her kitchen. As soon as she turned on the lights her passions surged.

She pulled out the recipe she wanted to update and began gathering the ingredients. She mixed her first recipe, put it in the oven, then began fixing something for breakfast. As soon as she placed that in the convection oven the doorbell rang. She walked back through the living room and answered the door. Chase stood in the hallway not smiling. "Good morning," she said.

"Good morning. Are you okay?" he asked, looking at her face carefully.

She nodded. "Yeah, I'm fine. What are you doing here?"

"I'm sorry for the intrusion. I stopped by the café this morning. They told me you weren't coming in today. I thought maybe you were sick or something."

"And I suppose they gave you my Key West home address, too."

"Actually, no, that information I got from my assistant."

She half smiled at the lame excuse. "And where did he get it?" she asked, knowing he wouldn't tell her.

She was right, he just smiled. "I'm fine. Today's my day off."

"Are you going to invite me in?" he asked.

"Oh, yeah, sure, come on in," she said, holding the door open for him. He walked in past her. The spicy-sweet scent of his cologne was heavenly and sent her insides tingling. He paused in the living room, looking around the small space.

"This is nice—small and comfortable. I like it."

She smiled. "It works for me. It's all about location, location, location. I spend long hours at the café, so this is my place to crash close by." She looked around. "It's perfect," she said proudly.

He walked over to the large plate-glass window. The top-floor condominium of the six-story building afforded her the perfect view of the quiet street coming to life below. "Wow, you have a great view from here."

"Yes, it is. I really love it here, but unfortunately I rarely have the opportunity to enjoy it," she said, walking over to stand beside him.

"May I?" he asked. She nodded. He unlocked the latch, opened the door and then stepped out onto the balcony. She followed. A warm breeze twisted and spun around them. "Yes, I like this a lot."

"Would you like something to eat or drink? I was just about to…" Just then a timer in the kitchen sounded. "I'll be right back," she said, then hurried to the kitchen, grabbed a couple of oven gloves, reached in and pulled her breakfast out of the convection oven. She inhaled the sweet, delicious flavors of the casserole. It was perfectly done.

"So, this is what you do on your day off," he said,

following her into the kitchen and seeing that she had been baking.

"Yep, I cook," she said matter-of-factly while peeking in and checking what she was baking in the oven.

"That doesn't sound like a day off to me."

"I enjoy cooking and creating new recipes." She poured maple syrup into a glass dish over a double boiler, then added pecans.

Chase leaned down over the baked casserole. "I don't know what this is, but it smells like heaven."

"Trust me, it tastes like heaven, too. It's a baked French toast casserole. Are you hungry?" she asked.

"I'm starved," he said, walking over to stand at the counter across from her.

She pulled two plates from the cabinet. She sliced and plated the casserole, adding a sprinkling of powdered sugar and the warm pecan syrup, and then placed them on the counter for breakfast with her unexpected guest.

After finishing his second helping and helping to clean up, Chase sat back down and watched Nikita move around the kitchen in easy elegance. "You're an incredible woman."

"Thank you."

"So, on your day off you cook," he began. "And that's it?" he added. She knew he was getting at something.

"I was thinking, since you're off, perhaps you'd like to join me today."

"Join you doing what?"

"Seeing the sights," he said.

"What sights?"

"Key West. Would you like to join me?"

She thought about it a few moments, then smiled and nodded. "Yeah, sure, okay, I'd love to."

"Great, so where do we start?" he asked.

"How about the Key West Aquarium? I have a friend there."

"Sounds good. Let's go."

She changed clothes, made a phone call and a few minutes later they were out the door headed to her car. In the next six hours they jammed in myriad island activities.

Their first stop was to the waterfront and the Key West Aquarium. They were met by Nikita's good friend, Leon Everett, the aquarium's consulting veterinarian. He gave them a private personal tour of the facility including up-close in the touch tank and shark tank. Afterward they took a glass-bottom boat tour along the living sponge and coral gardens. They enjoyed the spectacular underwater sights surrounding Key West in a motorized catamaran.

They took a skipjack around the uninhabited Mangrove Islands witnessing Key West's unique ecological system. They continued through the backcountry marine sanctuaries.

"This is stunning," Chase said. "Really, I thought we have incredible sights in Alaska, but these waters are unbelievable. You can see down through to the coral reef. It's amazing."

Nikita nodded. "It is. I love coming out here to snorkel and scuba dive."

"You're gonna have to show me one day."

"Yeah, one day," she said quietly.

Chase must have seen the pensiveness on her face. "What's wrong?"

"Nothing," she said easily enough.

"You got sad for a moment," he continued.

"It's just that I'd hate for all this beauty to disappear."

"Why would it?"

She looked at him. "When oil companies come into an area, things are bound to change."

"Oil companies like Titan," he confirmed. She nodded.

"Nikita, Titan isn't the enemy here. We're not going to come here and destroy all this."

"You don't know that."

"Actually, I do."

She shook her head. "I remembered hearing those exact same words before."

"From…?" he questioned. She didn't answer and just looked down into the crystal-clear emerald-and-aqua waters. A school of colorful tropical fish swam through the coral. Chase moved closer to her. "Tell me about him," he spoke softly.

"Who?" she asked, looking back at him.

"Reed Blackwell."

Her heart jumped at the mention of his name. She looked away again, wrapping her arms around her body. "What about him?"

"You broke up a few years ago. Do you still—"

"Correction, we didn't break up. He walked out, left me at the altar and married someone else. There's a big difference."

At the sharpness in her voice, Chase gave her an assessing look. "Do you still have feelings for him, love him? Do you want him back?"

"No, no, and hell, no."

He chuckled. "Good answers."

Excited chatter continued around them as other passengers on the boat enjoyed the visual spendor of nature's beauty both below and above the water. Chase and Nikita watched the school of fish dart and dance just beneath the water's surface.

"So do you have one?" she asked cautiously.

"One what?"

"Relationship disaster. You know, the one who broke your heart or the one who got away. Any regrets?"

"No, I don't have one, yet."

She looked at him questioningly. "No? Come on. Everybody has some deep dark secret past hurt."

"That's everyone who opens their heart and lets others in. I don't. I won't."

The answer was so definitive that it stopped her a moment. She knew she was steadily falling for him and he just admitted to feeling nothing for her. But this was how she started it. They knew it was just a casual physical thing between them. She was the one who changed the guidelines and started falling in love. "But how can you hope to find love if you don't open your heart to the possibility?"

"You're starting to sound like a romantic."

She laughed. "No, that's not me. But it doesn't mean I don't want others to live happily ever after."

"What about you living happily ever after?"

"I am happy."

"You know what I mean—family, children, the white picket fence."

"I have family—my nephews—and in case you hadn't noticed, I have a white picket fence at my cottage."

"What about a man in your life, someone who will love and cherish you, someone to come home to on long cold nights, someone to rub your back, touch and taste you in the middle of the night?" he whispered for her ears only.

She could hear the soft need in his voice. Her heart raced and her insides quivered, meeting his need exactly. He was right, she did want all of that and more. The problem was she wanted all of that with him. She turned to him and smiled. "Chase Buchanan, are you offering yourself to me?" she asked.

"Let's see how the rest of the evening goes."

"Sounds good," she said, smiling through her feelings. It was the perfect noncommittal answer.

Chase hugged her close then, and the rest of their conversation was mostly about the islands and the wildlife. When the boat docked, they walked along the beachfront and up along the boardwalk. As usual there were thousands of tourists mingling around the stores and oceanfront.

"There are so many people here," Chase remarked.

"Actually, this is a pretty tame group. There's probably only one small cruise ship here right now. Sometimes there are two big ones at port. Then it's really crowded."

"Wouldn't it be great to go to an island where there's no one around—completely deserted, total seclusion?"

She smiled. "I know just the place. Come on."

"Where are we going?"

"To a place with nobody around," she said.

"Where's that, the cottage?"

"Nope, we're going to Cutter Island. My parents are away so I know there's no one there right now."

They headed to Mikhail's private dock. Nikita climbed aboard a small motorboat and started it up. She navigated the narrow waters until they came to the Atlantic Ocean. She drove along the coast then headed out to sea. Twenty minutes later they came to a small island. She maneuvered through an interior basin then moored the boat as Chase jumped down onto the small dock and secured it. After tying the ropes off Nikita joined him on the dock.

Chapter 13

"Welcome to Cutter Island," Nikita said. "It's what you asked for—six and a half miles of total seclusion. There's not another soul around."

Chase looked around. The scenery was visually stunning. "It's like paradise," he said softly. "How far are we from Key West?" he asked, turning to the east and seeing no land mass on the horizon.

"You can't see it from here. You can't see any land mass from here. We're closer to the Marquesas Keys. That's a small circular chain of islands with a central lagoon. It's also called Mooney Harbor. And we're still about forty-five miles east of Fort Jefferson and Dry Tortugas National Park. Cutter is so small it doesn't show up on a lot of maps, but you'll see it on maritime GPS locators. That's the only way I know to get here. Surprisingly, there are quite a few dots of land around here. Most are reserved and protected national parks, but some are privately owned like Cutter."

She smiled. "Come on let's go up to the house. I'll show you around." She started down the dock toward the narrow pathway up ahead.

Chase lagged behind, distracted by the sheer beauty of the lush tropical landscape around him. But by the time he got to the stone pathway he noticed she had taken her top off and he caught up quickly. Her skimpy halter bikini top drew his immediate attention. It was held in precarious place solely by a thin tie at the nape of her neck that could be very easily released.

"It's kinda nice not having anyone around," she said.

"Oh, I most definitely agree," he said, licking his lips.

She smiled and bit her lower lip playfully, then turned to him. She began walking backward as she pulled his top from his shorts. Then she unsnapped and unzipped her shorts and let them drop. His breath halted instantly. She was wearing thonglike bikini bottoms secured by the same thin ties on either side of her hips.

"Cutter is remote but it's still totally self-sufficient," she began explaining, as if she weren't standing there nearly naked and making him pant. "There's a rainwater storage system that produces over a thousand gallons of water daily and it has two twenty-four-volt hydrogen battery strings charging photovoltaic solar panels with backup generators for continuous power."

They rounded a bend and a few feet ahead was a small elevated bungalow rivaling the surrounding treetops.

It was a single-story wooden structure with a wooden

deck that wrapped around the entire building. They went up the outside stairs and stood on the deck looking around. The panoramic view was breathtaking. "This is amazing," he said.

"This is Cutter Place, the only residence on the island." Nikita unlocked the door. "Come on in," she said. She led Chase into a bungalow with an open floor plan and a seaside view from every room.

"Wow, this is incredible," he said. "Who takes care of it? I'm sure members of your family can't always be here."

"There's a caretaker service. They do the upkeep for a lot of the private islands around here. There's also a security company that patrols the waters and the general area and sends daily email reports. Lately, there have been a lot of trespassers, but we usually get that this time of year. People think they can just come, party and hang out since there's no one around. But it's just like any other private home."

"What happens when they're caught?"

"They're often surprised when the security company comes along and arrests them for trespassing and breaking and entering."

"I imagine they are. So, why is it called Cutter Island?"

"I don't really know. I was once told that it got its name because this is where a lot of pirates would bury their treasure and if anyone should happen to stumble across it they would be cut to pieces. I guess we could change it if we want to, but it doesn't really matter. Come on, I want to show you something."

She got up and pulled his hand until he stood. They walked around the side of the house then down and narrow path. The sound of rushing water made her walk faster. "This way," she said excitedly. A few minutes later they came to a small man-made waterfall and pond. The water was crystal clear. She knelt down and reached into the cool water. "Isn't it breathtaking?"

"Yes."

She grabbed a handful of water and tossed it up at him. He jumped back but it was too late. She'd got him. She laughed and he shook his head slowly with a menacing glint in his eyes. She knew she was in trouble, so she took the coward's way out and just dived into the water. He followed right behind her.

Trying to outswim him was impossible. His upper body strength was too overpowering, so she dived underwater, trying to outmaneuver him. When she popped up and looked around he was nowhere in sight. Then she saw him and squealed just as he came up beside her. She tried to swim away, but he had her. They laughed as she surrendered to him. He kissed her gently, and then with an explosion of passion that nearly turned the cool water into a heated sauna.

He held her tight as she wrapped her legs around his body. Purposefully, he reached around and released the tie at the nape of her neck. Her bikini top sagged, then floated on the surface of the water, revealing her breasts, with the hardened nipples pointed right at him. He leaned down and licked her, playing with each nipple.

She pushed back, grabbed her top and swam to the side and got out. He stayed in. Seeing his shorts on the grass she turned to him and, smiling, slowly untied one, and then the other string holding her thong in place. A second later she stood completely naked.

He swam to the side and got out. He was already naked, hard, long and ready.

"I don't have any condoms here," she said.

He walked over and scooped up his shorts and pulled a condom out of his pocket. "I was a member of the Scouts Unitaires de France, the Boy Scouts. I'm always prepared."

She smiled as he approached her. "Only one?" she queried, reminding him of the statement he made the first time they were together.

They laughed as he took her in his arms and held her tight. He kissed her cheek and neck, and then her shoulders. Her mind hazed with the sheer delight of his mouth on her again. Then he dropped to his knees, pulled her close and took her nipple into his mouth.

She moaned as he kissed, licked and suckled her breasts. She arched her back and he nearly devoured her. Her legs wobbled but he held her too tight for her to fall. When his hand slipped between her legs she went limp and dropped to her knees.

She took the condom from him, opened it and slowly rolled it in place. He watched her steady hands touch and caress his penis, fitting the condom with ease.

"Perfect," she said, admiring her handiwork. "Now show me what you've got," she taunted.

"Nikita."

"Show me," she repeated.

His hands shook as he wrapped them around her

small waist and pulled her close. "Do you have any idea what you do to me?"

She squeezed his penis playfully. "Show me," she teased again, knowing exactly what it would do to him.

"Nikita." He grabbed her.

This time his kisses were ferocious, one right after the other in an insatiable progression of passion with unrestrained arousal. His tongue delved deep into the warm recesses of her mouth and she took all of him.

The intensity of his hunger and desire was beyond fierce and she wanted to experience all of it. Without knowing how or when it happened she suddenly felt the grass beneath her body and Chase between her legs.

A split second later he pressed into her, and then forged all the way. They were intimately connected. She wrapped her legs around his body and raised her hips to meet him. His perfect surge met her sublime thrust. With breathless desire, they made heavenly love until the swell of rapture took them.

Over and over again he thrust, and she accepted all of him until she climaxed hard and long, calling his name. Then she came again in gasps and shrieks. Her body relaxed, and he thrust into her again and this time she screamed as he kept the steady pace pressing in again and again. Each orgasm was an explosion beyond the last. Then she felt him tense and she thrust her hips upward, sending a quake of shivers through his body. They came together, one last surge toppling them both.

The next few hours they lay together as naked, free and unrestrained as the clouds in the sky above. Nikita learned too quickly that making love to Chase only once was impossible. It was abundantly obvious that she would never get enough of him.

They talked and joked and enjoyed the freedom afforded by the island's complete isolation. But without a second condom, she knew their kissing and playfully touching could only be cooled by a quick dip in the pond.

Soon the sky began to change. She cuddled close, nearly lying on top of him as he wrapped her up in his strong arms. She heard the deep groan of relaxed pleasure in his throat and closed her eyes. This was the perfect moment. She could stay here in his arms forever.

"It's getting late. We need to go pretty soon," Chase said.

"Or we can stay," she suggested as she sat up to look at him. "Sleeping here at night is like being the only two people left on the planet. It's so quiet—no cars, no cell phones and no drama. The only sounds are the waves in the ocean and the night birds and crickets. And it's completely dark. The only thing you'll see is a blanket of a billion stars twinkling above."

"It sounds amazing," he said, smiling at her.

"It is."

He shook his head slowly. "I wish I could stay, but unfortunately I can't, not tonight. I have to fly out to a meeting first thing in the morning. I'll be gone for the next few days," he said. Then, seeing the disappointment in her face as she stood up and gathered her bikini, he added, "But I'd love to be invited back again."

"Yes, of course, anytime," she said acceptingly. "I guess we'd better go."

After they dressed, they walked back down the path in silence, then after a quick stop at the bungalow, headed back to the boat dock. Chase released the lines and Nikita steered the boat back to Key West. The trip this time, she realized, was less exuberant as she marinated in her thoughts. As sunset fell around them, the water's gentle motion eased the boat back into the same slip as if it had never gone.

Once on land, Nikita drove back to her condo. Chase followed her back up to her front door. "I'd ask you in but…" she began.

He smiled. "No, I'd better not or I won't be able to leave." He kissed her tenderly. "Good night, Nikita." He turned to walk away, but she called out to him. He turned back to her.

"Chase, I have to know. What do you want from me?"

He knew exactly what she meant. "I don't know yet."

"Yes, you do," she pressed. "What do you want?"

He turned. "Everything," he said softly, "I want everything."

Their eyes met and held. "Chase, I love hard and I love completely. This thing between us can't go there."

"Why not?" he asked.

"A million reasons, but first and foremost, you're leaving and I'm staying. For that alone we need to keep this between us as just business."

He shook his head slowly. "It's too late for that."

"No, it's not. We just can't get more involved than—"

He half smiled and said, "Than we already are. Baby, we're already there."

"You know, maybe it's a good thing that you're leaving right now. It will give us time to regroup and make a new start. So if you come back…"

"I'm coming back," he said definitively.

She nodded accepting his correction. "When you do, we'll conclude our business. Have a good trip."

They stood staring at each other for a few seconds.

He walked back to her purposefully, his eyes intent and blazing with passion, and they kissed again. Then he turned and walked away.

That was all it took, one kiss, one taste. She knew with all her heart that she was in love with Chase Buchanan.

Chapter 14

The Titan company helicopter landed smoothly on the pad and four men got out and headed away quickly. Bane, Chase's grandfather's personal assistant, grabbed the briefcase and the dossier and led the way to the house. Andre shook hands, and then hugged his grandfather and Chase, then headed to the garage to get his car and go home to his wife. The last two men, Chase and his grandfather, Jacob Buchanan, CEO emeritus of Titan Energy Corporation, stepped away from the helicopter as it took off and headed back to Titan's main office.

Chase looked up and watched it go. It was good to be back in Alaska and to see his family again even if just for a few days. It had been too long. The good thing about this trip was that he didn't have to deal with Daniel's questions since he was in Washington, D.C., meeting with the Director of the Department of the Interior and members of the Senate Energy and Natural Resources Committee.

Chase turned in the direction of the massive family home, but his grandfather didn't. He headed in the opposite direction, away from the house. Chase followed him. The two men walked out and stood at the edge of the helicopter pad and just looked out at the lush greenery and expansive blue sky. Everything seemed calm and perfectly serene.

Nature was at its best here. Although mostly urbane, there were secluded pockets of undeveloped land just on the edge of the wilderness—this was one of them. The Buchanans owned a mountain, or rather the mountain owned them, and hence they would never leave. Here the land was pristine and the air was crisp and clean and along with the idyllic scenery. It seemed everything around them regenerated and was always brand-new.

"Breathtaking, isn't it?"

Chase nodded as he looked around the sprawling Juneau estate. It boasted spectacular panoramic views from its many generous decks and balconies. It was by far the most stunning estate of its kind. "Yes, it is."

"This is where life begins and ends for me." Jacob paused a moment then chuckled. "It took me damn near all my adult life to grasp what Olivia knew all along."

Olivia, Chase's grandmother, passed away a while ago, but Jacob was still feeling the loss and loneliness. "What's that, Granddad?" Chase asked.

"That you and my other grandchildren and soon-to-be great-grandchildren will carry this legacy on. In you

and your children and grandchildren and great-grandchildren, I'll live forever."

"That's a lot of responsibility," Chase said.

"Nothing you can't handle," Jacob said knowingly.

"Okay. I'll do my best."

Jacob nodded. "There's something very different
about you this trip. What is it?"

Chase shook his head. "Nothing I'm aware of," he
said.

"No, it's there—something very settled, very different. I can see it in your eyes. I saw it as soon as you
walked in the office. You were distracted during the
meeting like you were a thousand miles away. I know
that look."

"Maybe I'm just tired."

"Perhaps," Jacob said skeptically. "So, I hear you're
having trouble securing the Key West property."

Chase looked at his grandfather. "I'm working on it.
The time table isn't as desperate as Daniel would have
us all believe. It's a delicate situation and it needs a delicate solution."

"It always is where a beautiful woman is concerned,"
Jacob said, then turned and headed back to the house.
They went straight to Jacob's office. Bane had already
deposited the briefcase on the credenza and the dossier on the desk. Jacob sat behind the desk with Chase
across from him. "You want to tell me about her?" Jacob
requested.

"Who?" Chase asked.

"The woman who's got you all twisted around."

Chase looked at his grandfather, knowing there was

no need for denials and false bravado. He took a deep breath and answered. "Nikita Coles."

Jacob nodded. "I gather's she's the same Nikita Coles that Daniel has been raging about for the last few weeks."

"Yes. She owns the property we'll be taking."

"Do you love her?" Jacob asked plainly.

Chase didn't respond. He merely looked at his grandfather. Jacob's eyes were crystal clear and joyous. They were the eyes a man who had lived and enjoyed life and knew the answers to questions before he asked them. Chase shrugged silently. Jacob waited a few minutes. "Son, it's an easy enough question. Do you love her?"

"I don't know."

"You need to find out."

"It's not that easy."

"Of course it is. When I first met your grandmother, God rest her soul, I knew instantly that I wanted her." Jacob chuckled, and then coughed. Chase grimaced, stood and poured a glass of water for him. Jacob took a small sip while shaking his head, still chuckling. "Olivia, she was impossible, took me through hell and back and I wouldn't have it any other way. I knew right then she was the one for me."

"Granddad, wanting and loving are two different things. I want Nikita, yes. Being with her is like heaven. When we make love the skies open up," he said. "We get along great. It's perfect."

"You remind me of that in a few weeks when she finds out that Titan is taking her property."

"Nikita is stunning. She's intelligent, she's fun to be

with, she's wise and she's a million other things, one of which is fragile. I betrayed her. I let it go too far. I'm going to hurt her and I don't want to. But it's too late. It's already done."

"Trust me, nothing is ever already done that can't be undone."

Even with his words of encouragement, Chase knew his grandfather was right about one thing. As soon as Nikita found out about eminent domain she'd be furious. The federal government would take her property, pay her, and then turn it over to Titan.

"I need to go." Chase stood. Jacob walked him to the front door. Bane had already pulled a house car around front for him to drive to the airport.

"Chase," Jacob began as he and Chase stood in the open doorway, "listen to an old man who has been down this road. Love trumps everything. I'll tell you a little secret about loving a woman. When you're in love you know it. Love isn't about the woman you want to live with. Love is about the woman you can't live without.

"Now, you say you don't know if you love her—that's not true. You already know. Fighting it won't change what you feel," Jacob continued as he followed Chase down the front steps to the waiting car. "In the meantime, find a way to make this work. This is essentially out of our hands. Still, I don't want the last chapter of my book to read that I followed in Louis Buchanan's footsteps too closely and became a land-grabber. Make it work. Daniel isn't a patient man."

Chase nodded. "I understand."

A few hours later Chase was back in the air. This

time he was on his private plane with his GPS locked. He was headed southeast toward Key West.

Nikita washed her hands and glanced at the clock on the wall. She'd been going nonstop since before dawn and now it was time for a break. Leroy was humming as he put a special order cake batter into the oven, Russ was taking his break with a trigonometry book from his summer college class and the rest of the staff were at the front counter servicing the last few customers of the morning. It was the perfect time to step outside and get some fresh air.

A few minutes later Nikita stood at the café's front door, looking out as the construction workers continued going in and out of the building next door. It had started four days ago. A demo team had come in and begun removing carpet, lighting fixtures, doors, drywall and flooring from the building. The building was bare. She couldn't help thinking that it would look great if it were finished as part of her café next door, but today she saw firsthand the impossibility of that. It was official. She was too late. It was like the universe had given her a dream, placed the possibility in front of her, and then all of a sudden yanked it away.

Thankfully, there had been no significant changes to the outside structure of the building and she was happy about that. She had no idea who her new next-door neighbor would be or what kind of business it was. All she knew was that she wanted them gone.

"Hey, you okay?" Darcy asked as she walked up to stand behind Nikita just outside the café's doorway.

"Yeah, I'm fine, why?"

"I don't know. Everybody seems kinda gloomy and depressed today. It's like we all need an energy boost."

Nikita looked up at the overcast sky and heavy clouds. "Maybe it's just the weather that's got us all down."

"Yeah, maybe," Darcy said.

They both knew it wasn't the cloudy day. It was Nikita. She was the spark and energy of the café. When she was preoccupied and pensive, they all felt her mood. Today she was very pensive.

"So," Darcy began, "are you all set for the Teen Dream Center demonstration this afternoon?"

"Yes. I have everything ready to go. I was just looking at all the commotion going on next door. There's a lot of activity today. Looks like it's official."

Darcy glanced over, too. "Have any idea what or who's moving in yet?" she asked.

"No, not yet and the workmen apparently don't know, either. The area is still zoned for general business so it could be just about anything. They're probably setting up some kind of office."

"Well, at least that'll mean more foot traffic and customers for the café."

"Yeah, I guess," Nikita said, still distracted.

"Still, talk about lousy timing," Darcy added.

"Yeah, I know. Just as I'm ready to make my move, someone beats me to it. It's like they knew I'd been looking at it all this time," Nikita said.

"Who do you think it is? The property was bought outright. How many people have that kind of up-front capital?"

"Good question. Around here, not many, but broaden the scope and it could be anyone."

"You know I tried to pop over a few days ago all friendly-like and see what they were doing inside," Darcy said.

"How's it look?"

"That's just it. You know things are strange when even I can't get a little peek inside. I even pulled out my best Southern charm. They didn't budge."

"Well, I guess we'll find out sooner or later."

"I prefer sooner," Darcy said.

"Yeah. Me, too," Nikita said.

Nikita turned to head back inside when Darcy stopped her. "Hey, wait. Look, look, isn't that your architect coming out of the building? He's talking with that other guy with the blueprints in his hands."

Nikita turned back around and looked over. "Yeah, that's him. What's he's doing here?" she muttered.

"It looks like he got the job redesigning your building for someone else."

"Yep, I guess he did."

Then they saw Crystal Davis come out of the building. She was on her cell phone. A few minutes later Oren came out nodding his head as he talked to a man who walked out with him. They stopped, shook hands with the architect then, along with Crystal, he headed to his car parked down the street.

"Looks like we know who bought the building next door," Darcy said. "I guess that answers your question."

Nikita stared as Oren's car drove down the street and

stopped at the traffic light. "Yeah, I guess it does—and asks a whole lot of new ones."

"What do you mean?"

"There's no way Oren can afford to buy that building. He must be fronting for someone."

"Nikita, in Oren's defense, you realize he didn't know you had the money for the building."

Nikita took a deep breath. She knew Darcy was right. There was no way Oren would have known she finally had the money to buy the building for herself. But that still didn't make it any easier to see.

"Hey, you okay?" Darcy asked.

Nikita nodded. "Yeah, fine," she said quietly. But for real she wasn't. It was like the dream she'd lived for the last few years had suddenly ended. Her stubbornness had killed it. Had she sold the cottage months ago, she would have her building, but it was too late now.

Darcy walked back into the café. Nikita followed slowly. Since the early-morning rush was pretty much over and the lunch crowd hadn't yet descended, the place was calm and quiet.

Suddenly, Nikita felt it, too. Darcy was right. There was a gloominess in the café today. From outside she heard a car horn blow. She turned, seeing a familiar car stop in front of the café. Nikita stepped back outside and hurried over to her sister Natalia. "Hey, what's up?"

"I think my cold is finally here. I feel lousy. I'm on my way to a doctor's appointment. Can you watch the boys for an hour or so? I'm sorry for the short notice, but…"

"Don't be silly, of course I can watch the boys. We're

in between craziness right now so this is perfect timing." She looked in the backseat, seeing her nephews smiling at her. "Hey, guys, let's go hang out in the café and make come cookies for Mom and Dad, okay?"

They cheered, immediately excited. She helped them out of their car seats then held their hands as they waved, and Natalia drove away.

As soon as Nikita and the boys walked in, the place livened up immediately. They were the energy recharge everybody, including her, needed. The counter staff laughed and joked with them, and Darcy spoiled them like another aunt.

Nikita took the boys to the kitchen and as promised prepared to make cookies. Half an hour later, with hands washed and aprons in place, dough already chilled and ready, Nikita and the boys chose cookie cutters and began making giant cookies for everyone. They baked them and when they came out of the oven and cooled, they spread on lemon butter icing. Everyone ate and enjoyed their special cookies, saving two for their mother and father.

A short time later Natalia returned. She had a smile on her face that lit up the room. Nikita instantly knew the reason. Wordlessly they hugged. "I'm so happy for you, Nat," Nikita said, still holding her sister.

"I can't believe I thought I was catching a cold," she said shaking her head. "For real, it's not like I've never been pregnant before."

Nikita smiled and chuckled. "True, but not exactly the same installation process."

"You're right. In vitro wasn't as much fun." They laughed and hugged again.

"I have to call David. He's still on location. He's not scheduled to be home for another two weeks," Natalia said.

"I have a feeling he'll be back sooner than that."

"I think you're right," Natalia said happily. "Thanks again for watching the boys. I'll call you tonight." They hugged again, then Natalia left with the boys just as the lunch crowd descended and it started getting really busy out front. Everybody went back to work in a much better mood—Nikita especially.

She was thrilled for her sister and brother-in-law. They were wonderful parents and she knew that another child was exactly what they wanted. And now with her cousin Mia pregnant, too, the Coles family was growing in leaps and bounds.

She thought about her other sister, Tatiana, and her new brother-in-law, Spencer. Their wedding had been a quiet, private affair and they were currently living in London until Tatiana sold her flat.

She smiled. She was so pleased with her sisters' and cousin's happiness. Then a slow sadness filled her. She had hoped once that she'd find someone, but she didn't dare dream it would happen. Love just wasn't in the cards for her.

"Hey, are you daydreaming over there?" Darcy said. Nikita looked up. "Huh?"

"I asked you a question. When's Chase coming back into town?" Darcy asked a second time.

"I don't know. He said he'd be away for a few days."

"Yeah, but that was almost a week ago. He paid in full for your services and technically it went by the day and not by the meal. In less than a week you're done even if you never cook another meal for him."

Nikita nodded. Darcy was right. It had been almost a week ago. Like a teenager with her first schoolgirl crush, she'd been counting the days till he came back.

In that time he called her twice. And both calls seemed more obligatory than emotional. They talked mainly about the cottage and her connection with it. But what did she really expect? She was no match for Chase. He was obviously too good at this "just sex" thing. She'd played the nonemotional game before, but this time she got caught.

"Darcy, I think I'm gonna head out early. I need to make a stop before I go over to the Teen Dream Center this evening."

"Sure, good idea. We have everything under control here. Are you going home?"

"No. I'll see you tomorrow."

Nikita nodded then grabbed her backpack and left. She'd had enough for one day. She drove home on automatic. As soon as she got home she stripped down, took a long hot shower. She was headed to the kitchen when her cell phone signaled she had messages. One was from her very excited sister, Tatiana. Another from her cousin, Mia. The third was from her mom and the fourth was from Oren Davis at the real-estate office. She listened.

"Nikita, Oren Davis here. I want to meet with you as soon as possible to discuss your Stock Island property. With the taxes going up again this year it would be to your advantage to sell. I forwarded you my offer. It's firm. I will expect your reply within the next few days."

Nikita chuckled as she listened to the message a second time. Oren Davis was an arrogant braggart to most of the people in Key West. He boasted about everything, most especially his business and money. But this sudden interest in the cottage was totally out of the blue. It didn't make any sense. She knew he was no longer representing the Blackwells, so why would Oren suddenly be so interested in buying her little cottage? Who was he representing now?

Chapter 15

Chase arrived late afternoon, much later than he expected. Heavy turbulence over Colorado detoured the flight, and then a tropical depression extending from Louisiana across Florida's panhandle and down the western coast kept the plane circling over Key West for an hour. Now, the same ominous thunderclouds threatening above made it seem far later than it actually was. There was a storm on the horizon and he feared it was much closer than it seemed. As soon as the plane landed he got into his car and headed into the city.

He drove the streets of Key West with the familiarity of a native. It was a long flight from Juneau to Key West, giving him ample time to think. Unfortunately, all he thought about was his grandfather's warnings and comments. He knew Jacob was right; he also knew that there was no easy solution. There was no way he could have Nikita in his life and continue to work with his family.

He pressed the button on the steering wheel activating his cell phone. The first person he called was Nikita. The phone rang several times, then the voice mail system answered. He left a message. Then he called his assistant. He'd sent him back to Key West a day earlier. Kelvin answered his cell phone on the first ring. "Kelvin, I'm back," Chase said.

"We have a situation."

This was the last thing he wanted to hear. "What is it?"

"Daniel's coming to Key West. He's meeting with Oren Davis."

"What? How did you find out?"

"Oren told me, or better yet he bragged that Daniel and he had a business meeting coming up. Apparently, he thinks that they're working a deal together."

"Oren is easily manipulated. I'm sure that's what Daniel wants him to believe," Chase said.

"I agree, but it's still confirmed. He's coming here."

Chase slammed the palm of his hand on the wheel. This was the last thing he needed. Daniel in Key West was like a bull in a china store. Nothing good would come of it. "When are they meeting?"

"He wouldn't say exactly. But I gather it's soon—possibly by the end of the week. And one more thing, Daniel moved up the timetable. He had the architect go into the storefront earlier today."

"Damn, does Nikita know?"

"I don't see how she couldn't," Kelvin said. "The

workmen have been in the building next to the café for the last few days. But as to your association with the project, I doubt it."

"Okay, I'm on my way to the café."

Five minutes later, Chase drove down Main Street. He parked his car and then headed to the café, not bothering to even glance at the building next door. He opened the front door and breezed in with swagger befitting the Buchanan name. He looked around the crowded café and spotted Darcy immediately. She was talking with a customer. She turned, seeing him, then smiled and motioned him over. "Hello, Mr. Buchanan. Welcome back."

"Please, call me Chase. Is Nikita here?"

"No, she left early. Can I get you something from the café?"

"No, thank you."

"Would you like to continue your schedule? This evening is already booked, but tomorrow would be doable. I can email a menu to you in the morning."

"Yes, of course, that would be fine. But first, do you know where I can find Nikita?" he asked more anxiously than he expected.

Darcy smiled. "I'm sorry, she didn't mention where she was going when she left this afternoon."

"Okay, thanks," he said, turning to leave.

"Like I said, she does have another job this evening," Darcy said.

Chase turned back to her. "Another job, where?" he asked. A tense vein in his neck jerked and his expression was easily readable. He feared that Nikita had found out what he was doing and that meant she was furious. He needed to get to her and explain. Taking her land was a necessary sacrifice that would benefit the entire community. She had to understand that.

Darcy didn't say anything for a few seconds. She just stood looking at him. Then, she said, "She'll be at the Teen Dream Center this evening around five o'clock."

Chase nodded. "Thank you. I'll catch up with her there."

He checked the time. It was still early. Going to the center early and waiting would be ridiculous. He hurried out and back to his car. He needed to do damage control or everything he'd worked for would fall apart. He drove to the store to grab a few things then he headed to the house. He made a few phone calls, changed clothes, then got back in the car and headed to the Teen Dream Center.

Everything seemed different in daylight. Gone was the soft jazz music, replaced with the incessant chatter and laughter of children and teenagers. Mia Morales stood in the hall talking with a few teens. She said something and they laughed. She turned when he walked up, and smiled with genuine happiness. He wondered how long that would last once everyone knew his true goal.

"Chase, hello," Mia said with her hand extended. They shook. "Welcome back to the center."

"Hello, Mia. You look great."

She patted then rubbed her stomach. "Thank you. I feel great. So, how can I help you?"

"I was hoping your cousin was around."

"Natalia is out today. Can I help you with something?"

"Actually, I was asking about your other cousin, Nikita. Is she here?"

"Yes, she's teaching a cooking class in the kitchen." She looked at her watch. "It should be over in about thirty minutes. If you want, you're welcome to sit in."

"Yes, I'd love to."

"Sure, follow me." Mia and Chase walked down the main corridor though the auditorium to the kitchen.

"Does Nikita do a cooking class here every week?"

"She does two. It was once a week but the demand for her class was too insane. She does a nutritional and healthy lifestyle cooking class for adults and a novice cooking class for teens. We're so blessed to have her. She donates her time and the food. Since she's been doing the classes we've had to limit the students to only ten and even that's too many, but she does it and the students adore her."

"I'm sure they do."

"Chase, can I give you a word of warning?" she said very seriously.

"Sure."

"I don't know what's going on between the two of you. But know this, don't lose Nikita's trust. Believe me, it's not easily gotten back."

He nodded. "I understand."

"Good. Now, if I'm not mistaken I believe today's menu is lasagna rolls and garlic bread with fruit crepes for dessert. She also brings something special from the café. Today she brought watermelon salad." As they approached the kitchen the aroma of tomato sauce perfumed the area. Mia opened the door and peeked inside just as Chase's cell phone rang.

He looked at the caller ID. It was Daniel. "Mia, I have to take this," he said.

Mia nodded. "I'll meet you inside."

"Yes, Daniel," Chase said into the receiver.

"How do we stand right now? Do we have the property in hand or what?" he demanded. Chase didn't reply. Daniel continued. "A Realtor by the name of Oren Davis contacted me last week."

"And…?"

"He says he has the solution to our problem."

"I'm sure he did, and of course his plan, whatever it is, will also be to his financial advantage."

"That doesn't concern me. We need that property secured and your time is just about up. If this Oren Davis has a solution, take it. Use him," Daniel added.

Chase didn't answer. He peeked into the kitchen, seeing Nikita at the stove surrounded by her students demonstrating something. She was unguarded, cheery and carefree.

"Daniel, I'm handling this," he said, then disconnected the call and walked into the kitchen. Nikita looked up, seeing him enter. He smiled. She didn't.

Nikita smiled with delight as she watched her students walk into the kitchen for the day's cooking lesson. Ten eager faces instantly brightened her dismal day. She couldn't believe that she actually considered canceling it. But she knew she'd disappoint the teens. They really looked forward to the lessons. In truth, she did, too. The cooking classes at the center always revitalized her. Today was no different.

When everyone settled down the class began. She talked about various herbs and spices and how they interacted with each other and stimulated the taste buds. Her students smelled and some even tasted basil, oregano, thyme and rosemary. They also tested three types of mint leaves, pineapple orange, lemon and spearmint. Seeing the students try and figure out which was which was nonstop enjoyment.

Afterward they browned ground beef then sautéed and sweated onions, peppers, herbs and tomato sauce over low heat to make a tomato base sauce. Then, with everything prepped and ready, the class stood at the counter assembling their lasagna rolls. Some added a creamy cheesy béchamel sauce, others omitted it. They assembled and rolled the stuffed al dente pasta, then placed them in foil pans and put them in the oven.

Thirty minutes later the cooked lasagna rolls came out of the oven. While the pasta rolls cooled the students ate watermelon salad with fresh mint and feta cheese. They ate the rolls as they watched Nikita demonstrate making crepes. Although the class centered on inexpensive complete meals, she wanted the teens to experience something special each class. Today's menu was inspired by her cottage garden fruits. Blueberries, strawberries and raspberries took center stage in her dessert—summer fruit and mascarpone crepes.

She gradually poured a ladle of thin batter into the pan and slowly rolled it around, coating the bottom. As she described the classic technique, she looked up seeing Mia enter the kitchen. She nodded and continued the process placing the pan back on the low flame then carefully flipped the crepe to cook the other side. A few seconds later she coaxed it out of the pan, added the berry mixture with a dollop of sweetened mascarpone. "Who wants to try one?" she asked.

The students raised their hands excitedly. "Okay. Okay. Let's make this democratic. Whoever was the last at the stove making the tomato and meat sauce will be first for crepes."

The students lined up with small paper plates and forks. After everyone was served a crepe they went back to their seats and continued eating. Nikita glanced up at Mia again as she walked over, rubbing the side of her baby bump.

"Mmm, everything smells so good in here," Mia said.

"Come on over and grab a crepe."

"You don't have to ask me twice," Mia said. "Seriously, if you ever need a taste tester, I volunteer."

Nikita smiled then poured a ladle of batter into the bottom of the crepe pan. She swirled it around, coating the bottom. Then she repeated the action in another pan. Just as she was about to flip the first crepe over in the pan she looked up and saw Chase walk into the kitchen. She lost focus. The crepe flipped awkwardly and fell halfway out of the pan. It immediately began burning on the open fire.

She quickly sat the pan down, grabbed a spatula and tongs and moved the unsightly crepe to the trash can. "Okay, let's try that again," she said as she grabbed the handle of the second pan. She swirled the crepe around a few times then with a firm grasp, jerked her wrist and flipped the crepe. This time when she flipped, the crepe turned over and fell back in the pan with elegant ease.

The students applauded. She quickly filled the crepe with the fruit mixture, then added a dollop of mascarpone cheese, folded and gently placed it on a paper plate. She handed it to Mia, then looked up as Chase approached then stood beside her. The students instantly began talking and speculating.

"Hello, Chase. Welcome back to Key West."

"Hello, Nikita. It's good to be back."

"Would you like a crepe?" she asked.

"No thanks, I'm not a big crepe fan," he said.

"They're light, smooth and delicious," Mia said.

"I'm sure they are, but no thanks. I've eaten my share, believe me. I used to make crepes at my mother's café years ago. We stuffed them with bananas and chocolate and just about everything else we could think of. I got to be pretty good at making them."

"Really, well, why don't you show us your skills?"

He smiled. "Nah, that's okay. One chef in the kitchen is enough."

The murmuring grew louder as the students began to pay more attention to Nikita and Chase's conversation. She placed another pan on the stove, then pushed the batter toward him. It was obvious he was up for the challenge. He removed his jacket, washed his hands, prepared his pan, and then began making his crepe.

It was a disaster. He tossed a half-cooked crepe into the air and it fell apart midair. His second attempt was a failure, as well. He flipped the crepe and glanced away.

It missed the pan and flopped on the countertop. Laughter buzzed around him as he made his next attempt. It was perfect, and then he put on a spectacular show. At one point he made two crepes simultaneously flipping them in unison, then overlapping the crepes into the other pan. The students applauded wildly and Nikita nodded her approval.

The class had been over for the last twenty minutes, but the students stayed to talk to Chase. They gathered around asking questions about his travels and his business.

Nikita cleared the kitchen as Mia walked back in. "Hey, Niki, almost done?" Mia asked, leaning back against the sink as Nikita worked.

Nikita nodded. "Yep, I just finished. You ready to go?"

But laughter cut off Mia's answer. Both women turned, seeing Chase still taking center stage with the teens. "Looks like he's charmed the teens, too," Mia said as Nikita dried her hands.

"What do you mean 'too'?"

"While you've been working nonstop, he's been charming most of the citizens of Key West. Half the town's totally in love with him. He could run for mayor and win without even trying."

"When did all that happen?" Nikita asked as she tossed the paper towel into the trash can.

"Nikita, you need to get out of the kitchen more."

Nikita watched Chase as he interacted with the teens. They were mesmerized and seemed to hang on every word he spoke. A second later he turned around and smiled at her. "Yeah, I guess so."

"He's a natural with the kids, isn't he?" Mia said. "I wonder if we could persuade him to be a guest speaker."

"Ask him. I'm sure he would."

"Well, it's getting late and I'm beat. Stephen's on his way," she said, then walked over to where Chase was and told the teens that it was time to go. They gave a collective sigh of disappointment, then began moving toward the exit.

Chase went over to where Nikita was gathering her things. "Great kids. Some of them remind me of myself at that age."

Nikita went to pull her backpack up on her shoulder, but Chase took it instead. When she picked up the bag of kitchen supplies, he took that from her, too. "Thanks."

Nikita led the way back to the front door. Mia was there and Stephen, her husband, had just walked up.

Stephen kissed his wife, and then hugged his cousin. Mia introduced him to Chase and the two men shook hands, then chatted a few moments as Mia locked the door.

Nikita waited with her. "So, to what did we owe that honor?" Mia asked.

"What do you mean?" Nikita asked.

"I mean Chase Buchanan of Titan Energy Corporation didn't just happen to stop by the Teen Dream Center to flip a few crepes and hang out with a bunch of teenagers. He came to the center looking for you."

"You know that I'm working for him as a private chef. He probably just wants to review the schedule."

Mia laughed. "Oh, please. Who do you expect to buy that?"

"Fine, I have no idea what you're talking about then."

"Yeah, I bet you don't." Mia smirked as Stephen and Chase walked over. The couple said good-night, then headed to their cars.

"They're a nice couple," Chase said.

"They're the perfect couple," Nikita said as they walked to her car parked down the block. "I'm impressed. You have a little talent in the kitchen."

He smiled. "I'm not just a pretty face," he joked.

"I'm glad you came back."

"Me, too. I missed you," he said.

"Uh-huh."

"I did," he assured her.

"When do you want to continue the contract?" she asked as they reached her car and she opened the backseat. He deposited the bag and backpack in the car, then closed the door.

"This evening, right now," he told her.

"What?" she said surprised. "I don't have anything prepared."

"Then let me take you out to dinner."

"I'll email you some menu suggestions tomorrow."

Chase closed his eyes and took a deep breath and held it. "Nikita, I want you. Do you want me?"

Her heart went out to him. Every fiber in her being wanted to scream, "Yes, yes, take me now." But she held back. "You know I do, but I can't. I have to go. Good night, Chase."

He nodded. "Good night, Nikita."

He watched as she got into her car and drove away. As her red taillights disappeared around the corner, Chase turned, got in his car and headed back to the house. He pulled up in the driveway, got out and headed inside. Standing in the foyer, he looked around. The quiet stillness of the empty house was no surprise. It was just like his home in Alaska. Quiet. Still. Empty. He thought about Andre and his wife, Joanna, and then Stephen and Mia Morales. Seeing the joy in their faces made him want that happiness, too. He wanted it with Nikita.

Chase turned around and walked back out to his car. As soon as he touched the door handle his cell phone rang. He looked at the caller ID. It was Daniel. He considered not answering, but then changed his mind. If he was going to do this, he was going to do this right. He answered. "Daniel."

"What's going on with my property?"

"We don't need it."

"What?"

"You heard me. I decided not to take it. We don't need it. I've already contacted the Department, Senator Landis and the governor. I gave them my final assessment and assured them that the facility could be built without additional land. The Blackwell acquisition has given us plenty of land with which to continue this endeavor."

"That additional land could still be of value. I'm still going to pursue it."

"Then you can do it without me."

"What are you saying?" Daniel laughed. "Tell me this isn't what I'm hearing," Daniel said.

Chase didn't respond. "Damn, Chase. I hope this

isn't about the Coles woman, is it? I can't believe you're gonna turn your back on this family for a date. Yeah, I know all about the two of you hanging out. Oren told me. I'm surprised at you, Chase. I had such high hopes for you and your future at Titan. Now, I'm not so sure."

"I told you not to threaten me, Daniel."

"That wasn't a threat. This is. I'm coming in tomorrow. I want that property's deed in my hand by noon or..."

"Or what?" Chase said.

"Or I'm gonna have to make a very difficult decision."

"Why don't I make it easier for you right now," Chase said. "Consider this conversation my immediate resignation."

"What?"

"You heard me. I'm out of Titan. I'll finalize this with the board of directors."

"Whoa, now let's not take this that far," Daniel said.

"It's already done."

"Chase."

"Goodbye, Daniel." He ended the call with a Cheshire cat smile, turned off his cell phone, got in his car and sped away. All of the sudden he was feeling great. Losing himself and being swept up in the passion of the moment wasn't part of the plan. Neither was feeling what he was feeling when he thought about Nikita and their time together.

Apparently, Jacob was right. Love did trump everything and Nikita Coles was the woman he couldn't live without.

He had one thing on his mind—getting back to her.

Chapter 16

It had been a long, exhausting day and as usual Nikita ended it by coming home alone. Though she had to go to work the next day, the last thing she felt like was sleep. She knew laying her head down and closing her eyes would only mean she'd be thinking about Chase. She turned on smooth jazz, showered and changed into shorts and a T-shirt, then walked into the sanctuary of her kitchen. She turned the lights on and looked around.

This was the place that always comforted her. No matter what was going on in her life she always felt like coming home, going into her kitchen and creating something new. But tonight she just didn't feel like it. Instead, she poured herself a glass of wine and then stepped out onto the balcony. The sultry heat of the night surrounded her in a cocoon of comfort. Still, she wrapped her arms around her body and held tight. This was the time of day when it all seemed so real. The quiet loneliness of the night fell heavily upon her heart.

Falling in love with Chase wasn't in her plan. She'd hoped but the reality of happily ever after wasn't in the cards for her. She was okay with it. She had a career she loved and that was more than most could say. She was happy and if she'd never have someone to share her life with, she'd be okay. She smiled, thinking she could always do what her sister did with in vitro fertilization.

She looked up at the crystal-clear sky. A billion stars shone down on her. Then out of the corner of her eye she saw a quick flash of light as it sped across the sky, and then disappeared into the far horizon. Like a child with a birthday cake and candles, she closed her eyes and made a wish.

"Chase," she whispered. The light breeze carried his name from her lips out into the night.

Seconds later the doorbell rang. She turned, surprised by the sudden sound. Then she smiled, thinking her wish had come true. She hurried to the door and opened it excitedly. It wasn't who she hoped it would be. It wasn't Chase.

Natalia and Mia stood smiling at her.

"Hey, what are you guys doing here?" she asked, opening the door wider for her sister and cousin to enter.

"Hi," both Natalia and Mia said, hugging her as they walked in.

Suddenly, Nikita worried. "Wait, what's wrong? What happened?"

"Nothing. Nothing. Everything's fine. We're just here to…" Mia began, then looked at Natalia.

"Are you sure everything's okay?"

"Yes, Niki, of course," Natalia said.

"Where are the boys?" Nikita asked.

"They're hanging out with Stephen for a few hours."

"Okay, you guys want something to eat or drink?"

They nodded. "Something to drink sounds good," Mia said.

Nikita turned to the kitchen. Mia and Natalia followed. "Okay, now, what's going on with you two? It's been a long time since we sat around having an all-night girl talk," Nikita said. Just then the phone rang. "Wait a minute, let me get this," she said, and picked up the phone. It was her sister Tatiana.

"Tia, hey girl—perfect timing. You'll never guess who's—" Nikita stopped. She turned back to Natalia and Mia, suddenly realizing what was going on. Her sister Tia was back in London with her new husband, but still she was in on this. "Tia, I'll call you back."

"Niki, just because I'm not there with Mia and Natalia doesn't mean I'm not with them," Tatiana said. "Listen to Nat and Mia. Call me back later."

Nikita hung up the phone and looked at her sister and her cousin. "What is all this?" she asked.

"We're worried about you," Natalia said, sitting at the island counter. Mia sat beside her. She nodded her agreement.

"Me? Why? I'm fine," Nikita said as she opened a cabinet and grabbed two glasses, then picked up the wine bottle on the counter. Then she stopped and looked at her sister and cousin and realized neither one could drink. "How about some peach iced tea instead?"

They nodded. "We know that look, Niki," Natalia began.

"What look?"

"You're in love with Chase, aren't you?" Mia said.

Nikita stopped pouring iced tea and looked at the women. There was no use trying to fool them just like it was no use trying to fool herself. She *was* in love with Chase.

"Is it that obvious?" she said as she sat down across from them.

They nodded. Mia continued pouring the iced tea. "It started so simple and playful, like a game. It was just physical. It wasn't supposed to get serious. You know after Reed, I absolutely refused to put my heart out there, but with Chase it was happening and I didn't even realize it. It was all so easy and quick. What am I gonna do?"

"Does he love you, too?" Natalia asked.

"It doesn't matter. He's leaving."

"What do you mean he's leaving?" Mia asked.

"When?" Natalia added.

"I don't know, soon probably. I have a contract to be his personal chef for the next few days. I assume he'll be leaving after that."

"He could decide to stay. David stayed," Natalia said.

"David loves you, so of course he stayed. Chase, I don't know…"

"I do," Mia said. "I saw his face when he walked into the kitchen and saw you this evening. The man had *love* written all over him. Trust me. He's in love with you, too, no mistake."

"Still, he's leaving. He has to. He works in Alaska.

Can you see me in Alaska? And what about my business? No, my life is here. My family is here."

"Nikita…" Natalia began just as the doorbell rang.

"Are you expecting someone else tonight?"

"No." Nikita got up and went to the front door. She opened it and saw Chase standing there. "Chase, what are you—"

"Nikita—"

"You shouldn't be here," she interrupted softly.

"I know," he whispered, "but I need to talk to you. I…" he began, then stopped, seeing Natalia and Mia walking up behind her.

"Ladies, good evening," Chase said.

"We were just on our way out," Natalia said. Both women grabbed their purses and hugged Nikita. "Take care, sis. And for the record, I totally agree with Mia." She winked.

"Good night. Thank you. Drive safe. I'll call you tomorrow."

Chase said good-night to Natalia and Mia as they walked out and he walked in. Nikita closed the front door and leaned back against it, turning to Chase as he stood in the living room awaiting her. His eyes were filled with the same needful passion she felt in her heart. There was no way she could turn away from him tonight. Her days with him were counting down quickly. This might be their last time together.

"Just sex," she said in a near whisper.

"What did you say?"

She slowly repeated what she'd just said. "Just sex."

She tried to smile seductively, but her barrage of emotions betrayed her.

He shook his head. "No, not this time, not ever again. This is more than just a physical connection. We both know that. We make love, now and forever."

He came to her in an instant and took her in his arms. His last words dissolved instantly as he kissed her hard and fierce.

The intensity rocked them both. The relentless power behind his need for her took over. He wrapped her up in his arms with his mouth sealed to hers. She molded her body to his, feeling the hard, strong urgency of his arousal press to her stomach.

She rose up on her toes, then felt him reach down and grasp her rear and lift her up. He pressed her against the front door then moments later carried her into the living room and sat down on the sofa, letting her legs straddle his body. Breathless, she leaned back and grabbed the hem of her T-shirt and pulled it up.

He sat up, looking at two perfectly centered chocolate kisses. He licked his lips in anticipation. "Sweet, luscious, tender, juicy," he said softly as he gently kissed each nipple. "For days, you were all I could think about. Everything I ate and drank was tasteless and flat."

Nikita opened her mouth to speak, but found she couldn't. All she could do was watch as Chase leaned in and licked her hardened nipple with the flat of his tongue. "Hmm, you are all I crave. Just one taste is all I need."

He leaned in farther, holding her in place as he kissed and caressed her neck, shoulders, arms and chest. She was breathless from the loving assault. She grabbed and held tight to his shoulders as his tongue laved her with tantalizing licks, then he suckled her breasts, pulling and releasing in slow, deliberate pulses.

"Chase," she muttered, "make love to me now."

"Yes, over and over and over again," he said.

She pulled his shirt up over his head, and his massive chest drew her in instantly. She touched him, trying to memorize the feel of his body. She needed this memory for a lifetime. She knew no man would ever make her feel like this. She leaned back farther, then stood holding her hand out to him. "Come upstairs."

He stood and followed her to the bedroom. She walked him to the bed then grabbed a condom from the nightstand. She removed her shorts and climbed onto the bed and lay back. He dropped his pants and shorts, sat down next to her and looked at her body. "You," he said as he leaned down and kissed her stomach, "are so beautiful."

"You think so, huh?"

"Oh, yes." He ran his hand over her body. He began kissing her everywhere.

She closed her eyes, feeling the sweet sensation of his lips and the slight roughness of his five-o'clock shadow. He pulled and removed her panties, then she pushed, rolling him over onto his back. She climbed on top, covered him with the condom and then slowly impaled herself on his long, forceful arousal.

She rocked her body in slow, deliberate motions. The thick, solid depth of his penis filled her over and over again. She leaned forward, brushing her tiny sex nub against him. He captured her breast in his mouth and suckled, then gathered them both to massage them.

Now the frantic friction of their body and the insanity of his mouth licking her made her want even more. But she was coming too quickly and she needed this night to last as long as possible. She pushed back and sat up, leaning back on his thighs. His hands came up to cover her breasts. His thumbs tantalized her rock-hard nipples.

She knew what this was doing to him. She only had to look in his face to see his surging passion about to explode. But he held back, too. Then she moved quicker, stroking his penis in and out of her body. Each pulsating thrust heightened their arousal more and more. He grabbed her waist and held tight, guiding her up and down. The feverish pace gave way to mindless hunger. With one last thrust down she exploded and screamed. Her body tightened, her legs trembled and her hands shook. He rolled her over and plunged into her again and again. She came once more. Then on one last fateful thrust he exploded. That was all she remembered.

Chapter 17

An hour later she opened her eyes, knowing instantly that she was alone. She looked around her bedroom. Chase was gone. It was too early to get up, but she did anyway.

She went into the bathroom. Exhausted, she stepped into the shower and let the warm pulsating water stream down her body. She rolled her neck, letting the water flow over her shoulders, across her neck and down her breasts. She closed her eyes and stepped closer to the water's flow. The water streamed onto her face. It felt good. Then she heard the glass door slide open and felt the chill.

Chase was there with her. He reached around to cover her breasts. She rested her head back on his chest as his hands palmed her nipples. He circled them, then tweaked her. She gasped and arched her back. His hands dipped down the front of her.

"I thought you left me," she said.

"No, never again," he assured her, then nudged her shoulder and turned her around.

She looked up into his eyes and saw exactly what she needed to see. She saw love. He leaned down and kissed her tenderly as his arms wrapped around her. "Never again."

"Are you hungry?" she asked.

He smiled. "For you, I'm always hungry." He began kissing her, touching her, caressing her, tasting her. Her body trembled and quivered feeling his mouth on her— all over her.

The kiss pressed her against the tile. Then he picked her up. Her legs wrapped around his waist as he entered her. Slowly, he thrust upward into her body, once, twice, three times. She held tight to his shoulders. He stopped and looked at her. "Are you okay?" he asked, concerned.

"No, no," she barely rasped. He began to release her slowly. "No, I'm not okay because you stopped. Don't stop. I want more."

He smiled that lazy, sexy smile that always sent quivers through her body. "More, huh?" he queried. She nodded. "I can do more." He began thrusting again. Over and over again he pushed and pulled himself in and out of her body.

She held tighter and tighter until the blazing blast of rapture took her. The intensity was without measure. She called his name as he continued to thrust, giving her more and more until he met his climax in one last strained thrust.

He muttered her name over and over again. His body tensed tightly, and then shook rigidly with tremendous release.

Moments later he cradled her in his arms and closed his eyes. This was what he wanted to feel the rest of his life. She leaned her head on his shoulder as he still held her in place.

"That was crazy amazing," she said.

"Mmm-hmm. I think I like taking showers with you now."

She smiled as he slowly released her. "Yeah, me too," she said.

He lathered her body, then she lathered his. They rinsed, then finally stepped out of the large stall. She towel dried her hair, then wrapped another around her body and grabbed the body lotion.

He stood behind her at the large mirror, reached around and unloosed both towels.

"I think I like seeing you like this. Mine." The towels dropped to the floor.

She giggled. "Sorry, dude, I can't be naked all the time."

"Of course you can. You can be naked for me. We can be naked together." He took the lotion bottle in her hand and began massaging lotion over her back and shoulders, then down her arms. She watched in the mirror as he rubbed lotion down the front of her body with special attention to her breasts and stomach. "We should have a baby together."

"A what?" she said, surprised by his comment.

"Yeah, a baby, I like that idea," he said as if to himself as he continued to rub the flat of her stomach. "My baby right here inside of you. I like that idea. Two or three and then maybe twins. Yeah, and then twins again."

She looked into his eyes in the mirror's reflection. He was very serious. Suddenly, she began to wonder herself about carrying Chase's babies in her body. She allowed the words to roam comfortably around in her thoughts. It felt too good and too right.

"Cinnamon," she said.

"For a name?" he questioned.

"No. I smell cinnamon."

He smiled. "I cooked for you. I prepped cinnamon French toast with bananas and chocolate. Come on, I have everything all set up."

They dressed, then he cooked while she sat at the kitchen counter. When he finished they ate out on the balcony in the middle of the night. After the meal she sat back smiling.

"Mmm, that was delicious. You really are pretty good in the kitchen."

"Thanks."

"You know this is my favorite meal," she said.

"Yes, I know."

"But you never told me how you knew that."

"You were right before. I did know a lot about you, but not nearly as much as I want to now."

"What do you mean? How did you know? Did you have me checked out or something?" He didn't reply and she got her answer. "You had me investigated."

"I needed to know about you."

"Why, because of Mikhail? I know he does business with Andre and Titan and—"

"No, because of your cottage on Stock Island," he said.

"What about it?"

"Titan needed the land."

She swallowed hard. "It's just two acres. It's insignificant compared to the Blackwell property you already have."

"It's a strategic part of the new facility development. It's closest to the coast and we need the coast."

"What facility? Look, if you want it, tell me."

Chase nodded. "Titan has been commissioned by the federal government to construct a research facility. Our main focus will be the Gulf waters. We've developed a new element. I can't go into specifics, but it will greatly reduce the chance of another Gulf oil spill disaster."

"I don't understand."

"New oil platforms are being constructed between Cuba and Key West. Titan's new technology will identify, analyze and ultimately prevent or eliminate the possibility of another oil spill."

"So all this is to help Key West?"

"It's the first in a series of new programs we're developing for the U.S. government."

She nodded. Everything she thought about Titan was wrong. Perhaps they were the power-hungry beast at one time, but at least in this instance they were actually trying to prevent disaster.

"I couldn't say anything to you because if this technology were to be made public, our stock would go through the roof. Yes, that's a good thing. We'd all be multibillionaires several times over, but it would also cripple the energy industry. One test facility on the coast can be kept discreet. Key West is the perfect location."

"But if Titan has developed the capability to save the ocean waters from oil spills they have to do it."

"We are and we have been for the last year. We perfected the technology just after 2010, after the Gulf oil disaster. We were too late."

She nodded. "I understand. Thank you for trusting me."

"You're welcome."

"Take it. I'll sign it over today."

"What?"

"The cottage, the land, it's yours."

He nodded. "Thank you."

She yawned and looked up at the clock on the wall. "I can't believe it's still the middle of the night. I'm gonna be useless in the morning."

He stood. "Come on, let's get you to bed." They went back to her bedroom, undressed and got in bed. But they didn't make love. He just held her close until they both fell asleep.

Chase awoke to Nikita's kiss. He opened his eyes just as she was standing. He reached out and took her hand. She turned smiling. "Good morning," she whispered.

"Good morning. What time is it?"

"Too early for you to be up," she said softly, "I have a present for you." She handed him a tissue-wrapped package.

"What is it?"

"Open it," she said.

He did, and then smiled. "Thank you, it's perfect."

"I gotta go."

"Wait. Where?"

"To work."

"Wait for me. I'll go with you. We need to talk."

"No, stay, relax. We'll talk tonight," Nikita said.

"Tonight? No, I can stop by the café later this morning."

She shook her head. "I won't be there. I have a full day today. I'll be in the studio all morning and most of the afternoon taping the cooking segments for the local morning show and then off to the aquarium to help plan a function. So, I'll call you. What do you want for dinner tonight?"

"Surprise me," he said.

"Okay, I will. Seven o'clock?"

"Perfect. Call me later." She nodded, then turned to leave.

"Nikita, wait," he said. "Come here a minute."

She came to him. He sat up, smiled, and took her hand and kissed it. "Tonight we need to talk. There's so much you need to know about me and about Titan. But right now I need you to know one thing, that I love you. With all my heart. Nothing can and will ever change that. I've never said those words to anyone. And no matter what happens, remember that."

She nodded, smiling from ear to ear. "I love you, too. But I don't know what all this means. Our lives are—"

"Ours to enjoy together. We'll figure it out tonight."

"Sounds good to me. I'll see you tonight at the house."

Chase nodded and watched her hurry out with one last wave goodbye. He lay back in her bed and looked up at the ceiling. So this was what contentment felt like, he thought. He was happy. And most important of all, he was in love.

He reached over, grabbed his cell phone and turned it on. He checked his messages. He had fifty-two.

A second later his cell phone rang. It was Andre. He answered. "Yeah."

"It's about time you turned the phone back on."

"Hey, Andre, what's going on?"

Andre laughed. "Funny you should ask that question. I think I should be asking you. You have half the family calling you and the other half calling me. They want to know what's going on down there."

"What's going on is that I've come to my senses."

"Heads up, the family is furious and Dad is headed your way. He's not happy."

"Is Daniel ever happy?"

Andre half chuckled. "Not often. So what are you going to do about Nikita?"

"What do you mean? For the past three weeks you've been instrumental in forwarding the process of eminent domain on her property."

"I'll be deposing that first thing this morning."

"Good. I was never very comfortable with that."

"I agree. Have you told her you love her yet?"

"Yes."

"And everything else?" he added.

"Tonight."

"Good luck."

"Don't need it. I have love on my side. See you later."
He disconnected the call, then lay back and flipped
through his gift, a first edition, autographed copy of
Nikita's cookbook. He opened the front cover. Tucked
inside he found the deed to the Stock Island property.
He got what he came for. His job was done.

Chase wasted no time. After Nikita left he got up,
got dressed, hurried to the house, showered and dressed
again. Then he was out the door.

He told Nikita everything, just about everything, and
now he needed to make it right. She'd given him the
land; now it was his turn to give back. He called his
assistant.

"Hey," Kelvin said anxiously. "Damn, I'm glad you
called. Daniel has been driving me crazy. He's called my
phone at least twenty times since daybreak. He's looking for you and he's furious. He's at the Keys Gateway
Hotel, penthouse suite. Where are you?"

"I'm headed to the new property. Meet me there in
half an hour." Chase ended the call and steered his car
into town.

Chapter 18

At exactly seven o'clock in the morning Oren unlocked the doors of the Davis Realtors and Associates office and hurried inside. This was the day he'd been waiting for. It was a chance to prove he could dance with the power money. The plan was simple. Check, double-check, and then triple-check everything he'd already done. There could be no mistakes. Everything had to be perfect.

Working with Chase was one thing, but now, working with Daniel everything had to be flawlessly exceptional. This was his big chance. To date, Daniel was his biggest client and by far the most lucrative the office had ever had. Keeping him happy was imperative. If he landed Titan Energy Corporation and the Buchanan family, he could write his own ticket in the city.

He worked steadfast the next two hours. When his staff tried to interrupt, he abruptly told them he was busy and could not be disturbed. At exactly nine o'clock he called the Keys Gateway Hotel and was connected to Daniel Buchanan's suite. Daniel's assistant answered. Oren was told Daniel was busy and would return his call shortly.

Three hours later the phone call he was expecting finally came. He excitedly grabbed the phone seeing the caller ID announcing Daniel Buchanan.

"Good afternoon, Mr. Buchanan, may I say, it is a true pleasure to be working with you. I have every confidence that we will come to a very amicable and profitable accord."

"Mr. Buchanan will meet with you at the Keys Gateway Hotel," a woman's voice responded. "Your appointment has been confirmed for one o'clock sharp. Please do not be late. Mr. Buchanan's time is extremely valuable."

Oren frowned. He had hoped to speak directly with Daniel. Being put off by an assistant was degrading. "I'd like to speak to Daniel now."

"I'm afraid that's impossible."

"Do you know who I am?" Oren warned threateningly.

"I'll be happy to cancel your one o'clock appointment."

"No, no, of course not. One o'clock this afternoon is perfect, and please tell Mr. Buchanan that I am truly—"

"Thank you," the woman said, cutting him off.

A second later the call was disconnected. Oren bristled at the nerve of some people. He had more to say and she very obviously cut him off on purpose. He made a mental note to speak with Daniel about this assistant's manners. But for right now he was doing the happy dance.

Ever since dawn Nikita had been walking five miles above cloud nine. Being with Chase last night and this morning had done that to her. And then having him confess his love made her deliriously, unbelievably happy. She was about to get everything she ever wanted and the unbelievable truth in that changed everything.

It wasn't about the money he had or the job he had or the family he came from, it was about the man. She'd been fooling herself all this time thinking that she didn't need love and didn't want a family of her own. In truth, she wanted the happily ever after and everything that came with it.

She spent the early-morning hours in her café kitchen dancing, humming, singing and generally driving her staff nuts. Then just before the morning crowd began, she got two phone calls that had changed her day completely and she was even happier.

The studio shoot had to be rescheduled because of a breaking story and the event at the aquarium had been postponed. It was perfect. Now she planned to take the whole afternoon off, catch up with Chase and spend the rest of the day just being a woman in love.

Shortly before noon, Darcy came into the kitchen. She wasn't smiling.

"Hey, I was just about to get out of here. What's up? Are you okay?" Nikita asked.

She shook her head. "I think you need to see this."

"See what?" Nikita said as an icy chill shot down her back. She instinctively knew this had something to do with Chase. She washed her hands and followed Darcy out the back door. "Okay, what's going on?"

"Just wait here a moment," Darcy said.

They waited. "Okay, what am I looking at?" Nikita asked.

"Just wait."

Nikita looked around, centering her attention mostly on the building next door. Then she saw something not quite right. She saw Kelvin Simmons, Chase's assistant, come out of the building next door talking on his cell phone.

"Now, isn't that..." Darcy began.

"Yeah, it is. Kelvin. I wonder what he's doing here."

They stepped back slightly and watched as he hurried to his car, got in and waited. Darcy shook her head. "Seriously, I have no idea what all that was, but it's strange." She turned and headed back into the café.

Nikita nodded slowly. Suddenly, she remembered Chase's last words to her. *No matter what happens.*

At first when he'd said them she was too overjoyed by his love to get it. Now she feared the stark truth was coming out.

"Yes, it is strange," Nikita replied. She stayed a few seconds longer, then just as she was about to follow Darcy back inside she stopped. Her breath escaped in a slow laborious flow as if it had been sucked out of her. She watched as Chase came out of the building, got into Kelvin's car then they drove away. Nikita didn't move for a while. She just stood there, watching the car.

A few minutes later, Darcy came back out to her side. "Hey, you okay? Look, I'm sure this doesn't have anything to do with Chase. He was probably just checking the place out."

Nikita unbuttoned her jacket. "Yeah, right, of course."

"You had a call on the office phone. It was Wendy. She wanted to know if you listened to the message she left last night."

"What message?" Nikita muttered. She went to her office, grabbed her backpack and pulled out her cell phone. She replayed the message.

"Hi, Nikita, it's Wendy. Listen, I still don't know what the new owners want to do with the building next to yours and for once my idiot boss isn't talking. It's weird. Oren usually can't shut up when he lands a huge commission. Seriously, he gloats for cardio exercise. But now all of a sudden everything is all hushed. But he did say that he was purchasing some land for his new client out on Stock Island.

"Anyway, here's the interesting thing, the company didn't just buy the building next to you. They were interested in buying your building, too. I still can't tell you who signed the papers, but I can tell you it's a company out of France. It's that crazy? *France* of all places. Anyway, I hope that helps. I'll call you when I have something new. Later."

Nikita didn't move. The words refused to sink in. They just bounced around in her head, ricocheting like a pinball machine. A million things started going through her mind. After a while she smiled, shook her head and chuckled.

It was confirmed—Chase took her building now he was trying to take her business. She laughed, shaking her head. It was all a joke on her.

Darcy came to the doorway with a package in her hand. "Hey, what's wrong?" Darcy asked, seeing Nikita's shell-shocked expression.

"I just found out who bought the building next door."

"Who?"

"Chase. Titan."

"Oh, well, that's good, isn't it? He can sell it to you."

"I don't think that's his plan."

"What do you mean?"

"He's also trying to purchase this building."

"What do you mean?"

"I mean he wants everything."

"Nikita, no," Darcy began, her eyes wide with concern as she closed the door. "Look, I know all this looks strange, but I have to believe there's more that you just don't know."

"No, there isn't. I was a fool again."

Darcy sat down. "Why don't you take a few days off? We can handle everything here. Drive down the coast, to the mainland or better yet head over to Cutter Island and hang out a few days."

Nikita looked up. "No, I'll be fine. I just have to get to the bank." She motioned to the package Darcy held. "What's that?"

"It just came for you a few minutes ago," Darcy said handing it over. Nikita placed the package on her desk. "Is there anything I can do?"

"No, I'll be fine," she said.

"Um, there one piece of business we have to clean up."

"What is it?"

"The Chase Buchanan contract," Darcy said.

"What about it?"

"It's still open. He has two days left and if you decide to cancel him, he could void the contract, not pay or even take us to court for breach of contract. I know this is the last thing you want to hear, but…"

"No, you're right. I have to fulfill the contract."

"But what about—"

"Darcy, I'm a big girl. I've been left at the altar and now I've been conned by the best. Surely cooking a meal won't kill me."

Darcy nodded. "The meal information is in the email I forwarded to you. Apparently, he's having guests over tonight."

Nikita nodded. "I'll handle it."

Darcy got up and left without another word. Nikita listened to Wendy's message twice more then she listened to messages from Natalia, Tatiana and Mia. Afterward she grabbed the package off her desk, opened it and read through the paper. It was an official notification that her cottage on Stock Island was being considered for eminent domain. She shook her head slowly. It was official. She had lost everything, her café, her dream and her home. A slow, steady tear fell down her face. She wiped it away and left.

Oren gathered everything he needed for his meeting with Daniel. His briefcase was nearly bursting at the seams. There were high-end properties all over Key

West that he'd put before Daniel. A man like him would want nothing but the best.

Just as he was about to leave his phone rang. He checked caller ID, smiling. "Yes, Daniel, I'm on my way."

"Thank you for your interest," said the rude female assistant from their earlier conversation, "but Mr. Buchanan is no longer in need of your services. Your appointment has been canceled."

"What?"

"The situation has been resolved."

"By whom?" Oren demanded.

"I'm not at liberty to say. Goodbye."

"Wait. Wait. I want to speak with Daniel right now. Put him on the phone." His answer was simple and unmistakably clear. It was a dial tone.

Oren grabbed his briefcase and hurried out. He had all intentions of going to the hotel when he saw Nikita walking to her car. "Nikita. Nikita, wait up."

She stopped. "Oren, I don't have time right now."

"Look, I just wanted to apologize. I knew you were interested in paying off your mortgage and buying the building next to the café. But when Chase Buchanan made an offer to the bank, I had to take it. Then when he asked to buy your building, too, I just had to make the deal."

"What? What do you mean my building, too?"

"Hadn't you heard? He purchased your mortgage, too. He owns both properties."

"Why?"

"I believe he said it would be leverage."

"I have to go." It took every ounce of strength in her body not to pass out. She walked to her car, got in and just sat there. Her hands shook and her legs trembled. She was a fool. She trusted a man again and he betrayed her. Tears began to fall down her cheeks.

She drove to her cottage. As soon as she pulled up, she saw the one person she never wanted to see again.

Chase walked toward her, smiling, without a care in the world. He was a new man. For the first time in his life, everything was perfect. "Hey, there you are. How was the taping?"

"It was canceled. I worked at the café all day."

"At the café," he repeated. "I tried calling you. Your phone's turned off."

Nikita finally looked up at him and he saw she'd been crying. "What is it? What happened? Is it your sisters?"

She smiled and shook her head. "You can drop the act. I know everything. You got what you wanted."

Chase went still. She knew. "Nikita, it's not what you think."

"Funny thing, I just happened to step out back and I saw you and Kelvin leaving the building next to the café. You bought it."

"Yes. I bought it, but I have—"

"Then I ran into Oren and he told me the rest. Congratulations. You have everything you came for." She turned to leave.

"Nikita, please. I did this for you, for us."

"Don't, please. I've had enough."

"Nikita."

She walked away and he watched her go without stopping her. He knew she needed to calm down. But he assured himself that he'd make it right.

Chapter 19

Across town Daniel Buchanan stood on the balcony, looking out at the expanding city below. Key West was breathtakingly beautiful, but he didn't see any of it. All he saw was trouble. As far as he was concerned it was just another town. Like every other place, it wasn't Alaska. His only concern now was getting Chase back into the Titan fold.

Of course, he'd never admit pushing too far to get the property. It was a necessary endeavor at the time. But at this point he wasn't sure if he could stop the process from going forward. He turned and went back into the penthouse suite. His assistant waved and handed him the phone.

Before he could say a word, Jacob barked, "Daniel, I'm coming in now. I'll be there shortly."

"That's not necessary. I'll take care of this. Chase isn't going anywhere."

"It didn't sound like that to me. This should never have gotten this far, Daniel. Chase leaving Titan is unacceptable."

"I agree," Daniel said.

"Good, at least we're on the same page there. My plane is landing now. I want to see Chase and get this cleared up when I get there. Also, I want to meet Nikita Coles."

"Yes, as a matter of fact I do, too. I'll see you shortly." Daniel ended the call and looked at his assistant. "Find Chase now. I want to see him in one hour."

"I've already called Kelvin twenty times," his assistant replied. "According to him Chase hasn't checked in and he has no idea where to locate him."

"Damn. This is unacceptable. He can't just go off the radar like this. He's here someplace. Find Nikita Coles. It's certain that wherever she is, he is." Daniel dismissed her, then went back to the balcony.

A few minutes later she returned. "Daniel, Chase is here."

Chase stepped outside onto the balcony just as Daniel turned toward him.

Daniel glared at him. "Well," he said.

"Well, what?" Chase said solemnly, looking out but seeing only the stunning panoramic view around him.

Daniel sighed heavily. "Acting like an impertinent child not getting his way won't work with me, Chase. I think we both know you didn't mean that resignation remark. And even if you did, there's no way Titan is accepting it. You know it and I know it. You're a Buchanan and that means family honor above all. Your first and only loyalty is to Titan. I guess you forgot that."

Chase glared at him then smiled. "I just came from the mayor's office. I deposed eminent domain. The land isn't needed for the Titan facility."

"You did what?" Daniel stormed.

"It's done."

"Excuse me, Daniel," his assistant interrupted.

Daniel turned and glared. "Yes?"

"Andre's here. Jacob's with him."

Chase was stunned. Jacob Buchanan seldom left Alaska anymore. So for him to come to Key West was major. "Granddad's here?"

"Yes," Jacob said, stepping out onto the balcony. Andre followed, smiling at Chase.

Chase shook hands with them and hugged them both.

"Well?" Jacob began, "What's going on?" No one spoke up. Daniel huffed. Chase turned away and Andre shook his head. "Somebody tell me what the hell's going on."

Chase looked at Daniel. "Let it go," he warned.

"Fine, forget the land," Daniel barked. "Family is above Titan."

"She gave me the deed this morning," Chase said.

Daniel smiled. "How much did it cost us?"

"Nothing," Chase said.

"Nothing?" Daniel questioned. "That's impossible."

"No, it's not," Andre said, shooting Chase a smile.

"She loves you?" Jacob questioned. Chase nodded. "And what about you? Have you figured out what you needed to figure out?" Chase nodded again. "You love her."

Chase smiled. "Yes, I love her."

"Good," Jacob said.

"No, not good," Chase said, looking down. "She found out about me buying her building. She thinks I conned her."

"Tell her you didn't," Daniel said.

"She doesn't trust easily. She's been hurt and betrayed before, and it appears that I betrayed her again."

"Oh, this is absurd. Where is she?" Daniel said gruffly. "I'll tell her."

"No, there's nothing you can do."

"Like hell," Daniel said with his usual stern bravado. "Buchanan men do not get turned down."

"Actually, they do," Andre said, and Chase knew he was speaking about his first few encounters with his now wife. "Repeatedly." He chuckled.

Jacob chuckled also. "Yes. Now I remember my dear Olivia took some convincing, as well." He laughed out loud this time. "Actually, quite a bit of convincing. And if I'm not mistaken, Chase's mother wasn't exactly enthralled by you, either, Daniel. Neither was Andre's mother."

"They came around," he said.

"Perhaps it's the women who resist us the most that are the ones we love the hardest. Compliance is easy. It takes a real woman to say no to a Buchanan man," Jacob said. "Go get your woman."

Chase nodded. His grandfather was right. This wasn't over. "She's cooking at the house this evening."

"Really?" Andre said hopefully.

"Is that right?" Jacob added.

"I am a little hungry," Daniel added.

Chase smiled. "I'll let her know I'm having guests."

Chapter 20

The concept of running late was not in Nikita's mind-set. If anything, she was always early. But today was a whole other story. Her mind was scattered just as it had been all morning and afternoon. By early evening she did what she had to do to get through the day without thinking about it. She was going to see Chase tonight—that was unavoidable. One night, one last time, she could do this. She shook her head, not believing her mistake. How could she have let this happen again? He used her and she let him.

At five o'clock she'd gotten word that Chase was having three guests for dinner. She agreed, knowing she was going to prepare a feast. He'd taken everything from her, but she refused to give him her talent. She unlocked the back door and walked into her brother's house. It was the last day of the cooking contract. She looked around the kitchen, knowing instantly that she was alone in the house.

She brought her supplies in, prepped and cooked an astounding meal. She set the table, readied drinks, and then prepared sumptuous hors d'oeuvres.

At six-thirty she heard men's voices in the front of the house. She stopped what she was doing and took a deep breath. This was it. She could do this, she assured herself.

A few minutes later the kitchen door opened and Chase walked in. "Hello, Nikita."

She turned. "Good evening. Would you like to hear this evening's menu?"

"What I'd like is to talk to you, to explain."

"Why? You warned me, I didn't listen. You were right all along. I didn't separate business from personal, and you did. But tell me, why go through all the pretense when you were gonna get the government to take the land anyway?"

"I'm a Buchanan. I need you to see me for what I am, a Buchanan."

"Don't you dare hide behind your name."

"I *am* a Buchanan," he repeated. "I do what I have to do to get the job done."

"And I was the job all along."

He nodded. "Yes."

"And you got exactly what you wanted in the end."

"No, I didn't. I didn't get you in the end. Nikita…"

"Please. What can you possible say to me?"

"I love you."

"You don't love me. Remember this was all just a job.

You got what you came for. You got everything. What could you possibly want now?"

"No, I didn't. What I want is to be with you for the rest of our lives. Marry me, Nikita. Be my wife."

She looked at him stunned. Tears filled her eyes. "Why are you doing this? You won, you have it all—everything."

He shook his head. "No. I don't have you," he said softly.

She shook her head and turned around. He came up behind her. "Nikita, you once asked me if I had a relationship disaster, if someone had broken my heart. I said no, remember? I was wrong. I did this to us and I swear I will spend the rest of my life showing you how much I love you."

"Chase."

"There will be no eminent domain. The deeds are yours. The cottage, the café, the building next door. They were always for you. Say yes, marry me."

For a few moments she didn't say anything and Chase walked out. She turned around, seeing she was alone again. She looked down, seeing three envelopes on the counter. She picked them up. Inside were the deeds to the cottage, her café and the building next door. "What?" She hurried to the door and ran after him. "Chase, wait." He turned to her. "What is this?" she asked.

"A wedding gift, I hope."

Nikita noticed Andre and two other men standing in the dining room. "A what?"

"Nikita, this is my family. My grandfather, Jacob

Buchanan. You already know Andre, my brother, and this is Daniel, my father."

"She's lovely," Jacob said happily as he walked over to her. "Good evening, my dear. It's a pleasure to finally meet you. I've heard wonderful things about you." Jacob hugged and kissed her cheek. "Welcome to the family. It's going to be grand getting to know you."

"Umm, I don't... Wait. Welcome to the family?"

"Yes, welcome to the family," Daniel said, coming over to kiss her cheek. "We have a lot to talk about. You might want to reconsider the Stock Island property. We might still need it at a later date, but if you—"

"Daniel," Chase warned.

"Of course, we'll talk later. Welcome to the family," Daniel said again.

Andre smiled and chuckled. "Welcome to the Buchanans."

"Now, I understand the last time you received land instead of an engagement ring, so that won't do this time. You must have a ring, as well. It's tradition and I won't hear of anything else. Oh, and Alaska is the perfect location for a wedding. Think about it."

"A wedding?"

"She hasn't agreed to marry me yet," Chase interjected.

Everyone stopped and looked at Nikita, awaiting her answer. She was speechless. "Chase, could we go into the kitchen a moment?"

He followed her into the other room. "I'm sorry. They assumed you agreed to marry me. I'll talk to them."

"This is moving too fast."

"No, it's not moving fast enough. I want to start my life with you right now, this minute, this second. Say yes. Marry me."

Nikita took a deep breath. She knew this was her happily ever after. "Yes."

Chase grabbed her up in his arms and held her tight. There was a loud, rambunctious cheer in the other room. Apparently, her new family had been listening in. They came into the kitchen, cheering and applauding.

After hugs, kisses, congratulations and best wishes had been exchanged, Jacob stopped and looked around. "Good Lord, what is that incredible aroma?"

"Gentlemen, I hope you have an appetite," Nikita said.

"I most certainly do. Coast-to-coast travel always makes me hungry. I must say, something smells simply fantastic. What's on the menu?" Daniel asked.

Nikita smiled. "This evening I'll be serving you four courses, beginning with assorted appetizers, then a savory French onion soup, afterward surf and turf with crab-topped filet mignon medallions and grilled salmon, rustic mashed potatoes and baby asparagus. And for dessert, my delectable delights."

"That sounds delicious," Jacob said, licking his lips and slapping his large hands together.

"Nikita's food is mouthwatering. I can certainly attest to that," Andre said.

"I'll have your meal on the table in ten minutes," she said.

"Suddenly I think I have an appetite," Chase said, smiling and staring at Nikita. She knew exactly what he meant. "If you will excuse us, I'm gonna take my fiancée out this evening." He took Nikita's hand and guided her to the back door.

"Wait. What about the food?"

They turned. All three Buchanan men had descended on the stove and oven. They pulled the food out of the warmers and started taking the dishes into the dining room. "I think they'll be just fine."

Nikita nodded and started walking. Chase, still holding her hand, didn't. He pulled her back into his arms and looked around. "This is where it all started for me. Just one taste was all it took to know I'd never get enough. I love you, Nikita Coles, now and forever."

Nikita smiled. "I love you, Chase Buchanan, now and forever." She couldn't remember being any happier than she was this moment. All of her dreams were coming true. Chase kissed her and she knew this was the beginning of her very own happily ever after—now and forever.

* * * * *